Stuck with my BILLIONAIRE

AN ENEMIES TO LOVERS ROMANCE

KASIA KAIN

Stuck with My Billionaire

AN ENEMIES TO LOVERS ROMANCE

Kasia Kain

Contents

To my mom and dad...You will be missed Forever!

To Mert, thank you for always standing by me through thick and thin and our ups and downs. You have no idea how much I value our friendship and always have.

And to GOD, without you, I would not be.

CHAPTER 1

All bets are off

MAX

The heat of the Denver sun beats down on me as I step out of the black limousine. I adjust my sunglasses and run a hand through my hair, feeling as confident as ever. I've come to Colorado to compete in the most prestigious cooking competition in the world.

And I intend to win.

I make my way towards the entrance of the grand hotel, and my eyes are drawn to a woman walking towards me, her curls bobbing adorably with each step. I catch a glimpse of her bright blue eyes, and my pulse quickens. She is stunning. And then I recognize her as one of the other contestants.

My competition.

"Watch where you're going," she says after we nearly collide with each other. She was lost in her own thoughts, and I was lost in brazen ogling of her. She impatiently brushes invisible dirt off her chef's apron.

"I'm sorry," I reply automatically, trying to be polite but secretly admiring her looks. She is around 5'2 and petite, but her body has the most gorgeous curves. Her pink dress compliments those curves in a way that isn't too revealing or inappropriate but works wonders for bringing out her shape. Her blue eyes hold a world of mysteries for me as she looks at me, narrowing them as if sizing me up.

"It's fine," she says dismissively. I can tell that she is checking me out when her eyes discreetly rake over my physique. I smirk a little at that.

"What brings you here?" I ask her in a mocking tone, pretending I don't know she is a highly qualified chef.

Her eyes instantly leave my body and connect with my gray blue eyes. I see the annoyance flare in her blue eyes as she retorts.

"To make sure the prize this year goes to the most accomplished woman. Me," she says with a smirk.

My lips start to lift into a small smile at her sassy response, but I quickly stop myself. I could not deny that I felt attracted to her, but that doesn't mean I was in the right place or the right time to act on these impulses. She was another contestant, and she was going to be competing against me. I had prepared too hard to lose my focus, now, losing to a pretty girl.

I decided to ignore her comment and switched into my professional tone toward her. I hold out my hand and introduce myself. I'm not sure if it is more to remind myself that we are competitors and not friends... or to tell her.

"I am Max Myers. I'm also here to win this culinary competition," I drawl, confidence oozing from my voice.

I watch as her blue eyes spark with recognition, and a hint of determination crosses her face as she, too, slips into professional mode.

She takes my hand in her small one and gives me a firm handshake before she introduces herself.

"My name is Emma Castello," she says confidently and a little too sweetly. "Looks like it is going to be a fun week." Her innocent smile turns into a sassy smirk as she tosses her head. This woman was not going to go down without a fight, that much was clear.

I can't help but feel my pulse pound at her display of confidence. Despite my best efforts, I am intrigued by this girl. I have met several professional women, but this woman was something else... something more. I was into it. The determination on her face matches my own.

"You better watch out," Emma says with a mischievous glint in her eye. "I'm going to beat you."

I laugh, but deep down, I know she's a real threat. This competition is everything to me, and I can't afford to let anything stand in my way.

"This would be better coming from me than you. Baking is my forte. So, I would say that you focus on yourself and worry about how you will compete with someone as experienced as me," I say dismissively, trying to ignore the attraction I feel toward her.

I watch as she rolls her eyes and responds, "I didn't know we were competing against kids with such big egos."

I remain unflinching as I stare her down.

She waves a hand at me as if I'm not worth her time. "Don't worry. I won't embarrass you too much when I leave you in the dust," she says with another too-nice smile. Then, with that, she turns and leaves, a trail of jasmine floating behind her.

I relax my shoulders as I inhale her scent. What is wrong with me? Normally, women don't get to me this much. As we part ways, I can't deny that I've just met someone special. The fireworks I feel are intense. But I have to put that aside and focus on winning the competition. Little do I know, Emma is thinking the same thing about me.

The hotel lobby is bustling with contestants and their entourages, all vying for the attention of the judges and the press. I make my way to the check-in desk and flash my ID to the receptionist. She hands me a keycard and directs me to my room.

I let myself into my suite, room 145. The room is luxurious, with a king-sized bed, a flat-screen TV, and a breathtaking view of the city. I unpack my bags, take out my chef's jacket and knives, and lay them out neatly on the dresser.

As I head down to one of the show kitchens that has been especially set up to accommodate the chefs, I start to wrap my mind around the first challenge. In the kitchen I immediately find my station and start getting ready for the first round. It's an early round and I don't expect much in the way of competition. I refuse to look around, but I can't help thinking about Emma. I wonder what she's doing, if she's nervous, and if she's thinking about me. I shake my head and push the thoughts aside. This competition is too important for distractions. I can't let anything get in the way of my dream, no matter how beautiful the distraction is.

I start to collect everything I need for the first round: baking a cake. I want to keep it simple, but unique and a mix of peach and orange with hints of cardamom, ginger, and cinnamon will be perfect. I busy myself in the process of gathering all my ingredients and then patiently mixing them together. Baking has always been a way for me to relax. Since I was young, I have been using baking and cooking as a way to escape my anxiety. People usually take up habits like reading to escape the real world, but for me, I indulge myself in the art of creating new flavors and dishes. My mom used to be a chef in a popular French restaurant, and her way of bonding with me was to teach me how to cook. At the age of thirteen, I could make the most melt-in-your-mouth European style cookies that had people oohing with delight when they ate them. To me, it was simple. My mom told me that most people could not achieve just the right amount of chew and firmness, even after years of practice.

After my mom passed away when I was only sixteen, baking became my solace. I would bake every time I missed her, and before I knew it, baking had become my passion. I soon became one of the best chefs in my city and opened my own small boutique restaurant. When I opened it initially, I wasn't sure how things would go, but that small restaurant is now one of the top fine dining restaurants in New York, with me as its owner and chef.

By the age of twenty-four, I was already a billionaire, something most people do not achieve in their entire lifetime. I had published a hit recipe book and hired myself out as a private chef for special events for celebrities. That coupled with smart investments had set me up for life. I was not participating in the cooking competition Fire and Flame for money. The only reason I was here was to win the title for my mother's sake.

As a kid, my mom used to talk about how much she always wanted to participate in and win this competition but never got the chance to. When she finally did get selected, she could not participate because she was 8 months pregnant with me, and traveling was not an option. Even though she was torn, she never regretted her decision not to participate. My mother never made me feel like anything she did for me was a mistake. She always loved me, and whenever she talked about how much she wanted to participate in and win this competition, she never complained that it was because of me that she could not fulfill her dream.

And so for her, I would do this. I came here with one mission, and I would not leave until I achieved it. Whatever dreams she wasn't able to fulfill because of me, I would fulfill them for her. That was the promise I made to her. In a way, it was a final gift from me to her.

But somehow, Emma has crept her way inside my head, and now thoughts of her and her sassy attitude won't leave my mind. I find myself thinking about her several times before I stop mixing batter completely. I glance around at the small, strolling crowd that is watching me. I find myself looking for her familiar, round face in the sea of people. Then, I grit my teeth and get back to the task at hand. Emma will have to wait. Maybe that was the way around this—to tell myself I could have what I wanted with her *after* the competition. There's no way she'd turn down a winner... right?

On the second day when I walk into the elevator, I find Emma standing there already. I pause for a second, contemplating if I should get in or wait a few more minutes for the next one. Emma looks up and sees me.

She gives me a sly smile before saying, "Don't look so tense. I won't kill you just yet. I like competing with people fairly." She sniffs nobly and flips her curly hair, a habit I've already picked up on that I find impossibly cute.

As much as I am impressed by her, I am also annoyed by how relaxed and sassy she is around me. I have no doubt that I am an intimidating man, and people at my restaurant cower in front of me. But somehow, this girl has the nerve to stand there and mock me, even as I give her a death glare.

I decide to just get in and get this over with. The sooner she is away from me, the better. I step inside the elevator and stand in one corner while she leans against the other corner of the elevator. I take that time to check her out, hoping to throw her off her A-game.

She looks just as gorgeous as she did yesterday, but today she is wearing a bright red dress that compliments her golden skin. The dress reaches her thighs, putting those gorgeous legs on display. I want nothing more than for her to wrap them around my waist as I kiss her neck. The thought of her pressed up against the wall as I cage her in my arms and rain seductive kisses down her neck enters my mind, and I can already feel my cock getting hard.

Jesus, I need to stop thinking of her like this. I quickly avert my eyes and look down at my watch, trying to act indifferent when I feel her eyes on me. I subtly lift my eyes to see what she is looking at and to see her checking me out, too. The fact that she is checking me out is proof that I am not the only one who is attracted to her. I smirk at the realization that she can't help but keep her eyes on me whenever she is in the same place as me.

Before I can mock her about this, the elevator stops, and another guy steps in. He pauses for a second when he sees me and Emma standing there, but then shrugs and comes to stand in between us. His shoulder brushes Emma's, and when she realizes it, she turns to him and gives him a warm smile.

My jaw clenches at that, even though I know I have no right to be mad or annoyed at this. Emma isn't my girlfriend. She is nothing but my competitor, and I need to get my head in the game, but something about that guy standing so close to her irks me. I try to ignore the feeling. I do not understand what the hell is wrong with me. I have never felt this way for any girl, so why am I suddenly acting like this for her? What kind of spell has she put on me? As if in response to my thoughts, I catch the intoxicating scent of jasmine.

As soon as the elevator stops, I push past the guy standing next to Emma and storm out, not wanting to be anywhere near this troublesome girl. She seemed to bring out a side of me no one has ever brought out of me before, and I don't like it one bit.

I have one purpose for being here, and that was to fulfill my mother's dreams and make her proud, and I am going to forget about everything else but that. I need to remember that this girl is my enemy, not a friend. I brush away the thoughts of her from my head and walk towards the exit to get some fresh air.

But as the days go on and the rounds progress, I find myself drawn to her more and more. She's a worthy competitor, with skills and ideas that challenge me in ways I never thought possible. Where my cooking has depth in each of its flavor profiles and a certain moodiness to the flavors I choose, her dishes are zesty, tangy, and full of surprise. And as the tension between us grows, I realize that this competition is about more than just cooking. it is about finding out who I am and what I'm willing to risk for the person I want to be with. All bets are off, and I'm not ready for the stakes.

CHAPTER 2

Sweet Competition

EMMA

I re-check the time as I mix the icing for my cupcakes. The cupcakes have to be pulled out in exactly seven minutes, otherwise they will not have the fluffy texture I want them to have. I keep my attention on the clock even as I mix different food colors in my icing to get the perfect lilac shade. As soon as I am done mixing my icing, I put it in the piping bag. Just as I set the piping bag down on the counter, I check the time and realize it has been six minutes. I rush to the oven and keep my eyes trained on the clock, waiting for it to be exactly seven minutes before I open the oven. I count down for thirty seconds and pull the vanilla cupcakes out of the oven. They are flavored with my super-secret ingredient that makes them more than just vanilla.

The smell of freshly baked cupcakes instantly infiltrates the room. I inhale deeply, smiling in contentment at the cupcakes in my hand. They are the perfect shade of light golden brown. I quickly walk back to my counter, set the cupcake pan down, and wait for it to cool a bit before I take them out of the tray.

I hear an amused snort from behind me as I wait for the cupcakes to cool down. I turn around to find the broad frame of Max leaning against the wall as he looks at me with a playful expression. Unable to resist, my eyes trail down his body. I take note of how his biceps flex as he folds his arms across his chest. There is no doubt in my mind that Max is gorgeous. He looks to be in his late thirties with straight black hair that falls over his forehead and a jawline that could cut glass. His gray eyes are intense as he looks at me, even though amusement is still visible in them.

I watch as his pink lips, which look so soft that I can't help but wonder what it would feel like to kiss them, lift into a smirk. The arrogance smeared on his gorgeous features pulls me out of a trance as I realize I have yet again been caught checking him out. Damn it, this really isn't doing me any favors. I need to get a grip on myself.

I quickly look away from him and narrow my eyes in annoyance.

"I am starting to think you are obsessed with me or something. Wherever I go, you turn up." I ask as I turn towards him, my tone light but my gaze challenging.

"Maybe it is you who keeps showing up wherever I go," he says with a shrug.

"Dream on. I have better things to do than follow around some grandpa who thinks he is better than anyone else," I say as I roll my eyes, even though he and I both know that he is indeed better looking than most people here, and neither is he a grandpa, but I would never admit to any of those things.

"I do not just *think* I am better than everyone else in this competition. I *know* I am," he says confidently.

I snort at his words. I know he's just playing a mind game with me, but honestly, he's pretty bad at it.

"Whatever." With that one word I let him know I'm done with the conversation. That seems to turn on his energy even more and his eyes sizzle into mine. "Look, I don't have time to waste arguing with you. Stop beating around the bush and wasting my time. What do you want?" I ask him, annoyance evident in my voice.

"Is that the only thing you know how to bake?" he asks suddenly, his eyes looking at my cupcakes. He inhales deeply and I worry he'll pick up the scent of my secret ingredient.

"What is that supposed to mean?" I snap at him, getting defensive as soon as those words slip out of his mouth. Decadent cupcakes are part of my brand as a chef.

His expression changes from a smirk for a moment, realizing that I had actually taken offense to what he had said. But he quickly masks his face in a calm, relaxed expression.

"All I mean is that the first time I met you, you were holding cupcakes, and again today, you are baking the same thing. You do know that there is more to baking than just knowing how to make a few simple vanilla cupcakes, right? Because if this is what you are here to offer, then this competition is going to be a piece of cake for me—oh, wait, sorry, a piece of cupcake," he says with a mocking lilt in his voice.

My hands ball into fists as I hear his condescending words, reminding me of all the things I had to endure before. My father's snarky, mean comments crash into me. He used to say more or less the exact same thing. My father himself is a famous patisserie chef, and he owns one of the most well-known bakeries in the entire world. There is hardly anyone who doesn't know what an incredible chef Marcus Castello is. But no one knows what a horrible father he is to his daughter. Me.

As a kid, I looked up to my father and his skills. He was talented, and my mom talked about how she knew from the first time he cooked for her that he would make it big one day. And he had. At the age of thirty, he already owned his own bakery and had a steady income, so he never had to be worried about money. But then, all of a sudden, he was no longer satisfied with what he had. He wanted more and more with every passing day. Soon, my father was replaced with a man who only cared about his career.

As a way to repair things and connect with him again, I tried to follow in his footsteps and start cooking and baking, too, but instead of hyping me up and motivating me, all I got from him was harsh criticism. No matter what I did, he was never satisfied, nor was he ever impressed.

The cupcakes were too soft or not golden enough. My cakes just didn't taste good, and my cookies lacked the buttery texture he could easily add to his own cookies.

Eventually, I gave up, knowing that there was no chance for me to win his approval, or his love. But along the way, I found myself falling in love with the whole thing. I found myself enjoying my time as I baked and tried different recipes, mixing bright and cheerful flavors to create something unique.

But when I saw the chance to participate in the Fire and Flame competition, which is one of the most prestigious cooking competitions in the world, I knew at that moment that I had to try my luck. Not just because I love cooking and want to win this competition, nor am I doing this for the money. I want to win this because this is the one cooking competition my father has tried to win his entire life but never succeeded.

When I learned that I had been selected for this competition, I could not believe it, but I had to put a tamper on my feelings. Getting selected is not my endgame. Winning is. I am going to prove to my father that I am better than him and that no matter how much he tries to put me down, I'll still succeed.

And neither will Max's words demotivate me or put me down. I do not care if he thinks that just because he owns his own restaurant that means he can get everything he wants and that everyone is beneath him. I will prove him wrong by winning this competition.

"Don't worry yourself about what I can and can't do. Just focus on your own baking because once I win this competition, you will be begging me for my secrets. And I won't give them to you," I retort confidently, even though I am still a little disoriented by all the bad memories his words have brought back to me.

Before he can reply, I continue.

"If you are done here, please leave. This kitchen is occupied for now, and I really do not want you here. There's the door," I tell him, pointing my head towards the door.

I watch as his jaw clenches at my dismissal, but I do not back down. It doesn't matter that I am attracted to him or that whenever he is near my heart starts beating like crazy. All that matters is that this guy is my competitor, and I can't ever forget that.

"Secrets, huh? Interesting." His eyes rake over my cupcakes a little too thoroughly before he looks through the ingredients I still have sitting out on the counter. I laugh to myself. My secret ingredient is never on display. It's safe in its innocent-looking little jar, intentionally mislabeled. "Well, I may have a secret or two of my own," he says softly before he struts out of the room.

My eyes narrow on his retreating figure. Who the hell does this guy think he is?

I know very well that Max is a formidable opponent. He has a natural talent for baking and a confident demeanor that puts the other contestants on edge. But I refuse to let him intimidate me. I have worked hard for this moment, and I am not going to let anyone get in my way. So far, I am breezing through the early rounds, outperforming the other contestants and watching them get eliminated one by one. When I'm not competing, I'm in one of the kitchens practicing. I may not have the early success that Max does with his restaurant, but I have drive. And that has to be enough.

CHAPTER 3

Room with A View

MAX

I walk towards my room after a long day of practicing my bake for the next round. A long, warm shower is all I need.

"145...145..." I absently mumble the room number as I walk through the corridor. "There it is." I swipe the card and open the door only to come face to face with Emma, in a towel, coming out of the bathroom.

"I-"

"You-" We begin simultaneously, pointing at each other. Emma holds the towel close as she tries to find her clothes. We stand there for a moment, awkwardly avoiding each other's gaze. I can't help but notice how her wet hair clings to her shoulders, and her flushed cheeks make her look even more beautiful.

"What are you doing here?" I ask.

"What am I doing? What are *you* doing here!" Emma retorts.

"Well, this is my room." I exclaim, chuckling.

"No, it is my room," Emma argues, holding up her keycard to show me the number 145.

"That's impossible. I was given this room at check-in days ago," I say, pulling out my keycard and showing her the same number.

We both stare at each other, unsure of what to do next. "This must be some kind of mix-up," I suggest, trying to diffuse the tension, keeping my gaze off her toned legs.

"My room had an issue with the plumbing. So, they just gave me this one today. I'm so confused. Let's go ask the front desk," Emma suggests, suddenly flustered as she looks at me. I keep looking at her, and she keeps looking at me, gesturing with her eyes to leave.

"What," I begin, only to register a second later that she is asking me to leave so she can change.

I nod in understanding and quickly grab my things before leaving the room.

Emma comes out, and we make our way to the front desk, still wrapped in our thoughts.

"Excuse me, there seems to be a problem with our room assignments," Emma says to the front desk staff.

The agent looks up from their computer screen and greets us with a smile. "What seems to be the issue?"

"We were both assigned to room 145," I explain. "But I was given that room first. We're here for the baking competition so..."

Emma glances at me impatiently as if I'm rambling.

The agent furrows their brow and begins typing on the keyboard. "I apologize for the inconvenience. Let's see what we can do."

Emma and I exchange awkward glances while waiting for the agent to sort things out.

After a few minutes, the agent turns back to us. "It looks like there was a mistake in our system. Both of you were indeed assigned to room 145. I'm afraid the hotel is fully booked because of the competition, so no other rooms are available."

"What about my old room? The one with the plumbing problem?" Emma asks hopefully.

"That one is on our do not rent list. I'm sorry. The flooring was flooded and will need to be replaced. We have no rooms available."

Emma and I both let out a sigh of frustration. "So, what do we do now?" she asks.

The agent thinks for a moment before suggesting, "Perhaps you two could share the room? We can bring in a rollaway bed if needed."

Emma and I both hesitate for a moment before reluctantly agreeing. We are both here to compete, not lounge around in the room, anyway. It's unlikely we'll be in the room at all other than to sleep.

"This is ridiculous," she says, throwing her bags on the bed once we are back in my room. "I can't believe they messed up like that."

"I know," I say, trying to keep the frustration out of my voice. "But we'll just have to make the best of it."

She raises an eyebrow at me. "Make the best of it? How are we supposed to do that? We're supposed to be competing against each other."

I sit down on the other bed and shrug. "I don't know. Maybe we can get to know each other better. Find out what makes us tick as chefs."

Emma snorts. "I highly doubt that."

I chuckle. "Come on. It can't hurt to try. We might even learn something from each other."

Emma crosses her arms and looks at me skeptically. "Fine, but do not expect me to share any of my secret recipes with you."

I grin. There she goes with that word "secret" again. "I would not dream of it."

"Well, I'm going to shower," I say. "I'll be quick."

As I head towards the bathroom, I can feel her eyes on me, studying me. I wonder what she's thinking.

After my shower, I find Emma sitting on the bed and flipping through a magazine.

"Hey, mind if I join you?" I ask, sitting down next to her.

She looks up and smiles. "Sure, go ahead."

As I settle in next to her, I can't help but notice the rollaway bed that has been set up on the other side of the room. It is a stark reminder that we're sharing a room and that tomorrow we'll be competing against each other once again.

We sit silently for a while, neither of us sure how to continue the conversation. Emma glances up for a brief moment and looks outside the window.

"It's snowing..." she states, surprise in her voice. "It was so sunny the other day."

"That's Denver in the spring, all right," I chuckle.

I turn my head to follow her gaze, and sure enough, a light snowfall has begun outside. I make a mental note to see if the snow brings any extra humidity into the air as the heaters work to keep the building warm. If so, I'll have to adjust the liquid content of all my recipes. I wonder if Emma accounts for this type of nuisance in her baking.

"It's pretty," I say, feeling a bit awkward at the sudden silence.

Emma breaks the silence. "You know, whenever it would snow like this, my grandma would make hot chocolate and cookies for me. So, snow always reminds me of her," she says wistfully.

I smile at her, happy to have something to talk about. "That's sweet. Did your grandma have a secret recipe for hot chocolate?"

Emma laughs softly. "Not really. She just knew how to make it extra creamy. And she always topped it off with a generous dollop of whipped cream. Homemade, of course."

"Of course," I nod, picturing the scene in my mind. "Sounds amazing. My mom used to make hot cocoa for us, too, but she would add a pinch of ginger to it. It gave it a nice kick."

Emma looks intrigued. "I've never tried that before. I'll have to give it a shot."

Emma smiles, and I ask, trying to keep the conversation going. "So, I'm guessing she is why you became a chef?"

Emma pauses for a second but quickly masks her expression and nods, "Yeah, she was the one who first taught me how to cook. I remember spending hours in the kitchen with her, baking cookies and cakes, making homemade pasta, and learning all sorts of recipes from around the world."

I can't help but feel like she is hiding something from me. The way she completely froze when I asked her about this seems suspicious and I can't help but feel like she is lying about her grandmother being the one who influenced her to start baking. But before I can probe deeper, she changes the topic.

"So, what about you?" Emma asks, interrupting my thoughts. "What's your story?"

I hesitate for a moment before deciding to share. "My mom was a chef," I say. "I always wanted to follow in her footsteps. But when she passed away, I felt like I had to prove myself even more."

Emma's expression softens. "I'm sorry for your loss," she says quietly.

I nod, grateful for her sympathy. "But I also know that cooking is my passion. It is what I love to do."

We fall quiet for a while, our eyes darting to sneak glances at each other while trying to pretend there is no attraction between us. Emma's cheeks have a beautiful flush to them, and I wonder what she's thinking.

Emma suddenly gets up from the bed and reaches into one of her bags. "You don't have any more baking to do today, right?"

I shake my head.

"Good. Well, I think you'll like this," she announces with a smile, pulling out a bottle of wine from one of her carry-on bags. "It is a family recipe. From one of my dad's vineyards."

I raise an eyebrow in surprise. "Really? That's impressive."

As Emma pours the wine, I can't help but feel my heart racing with anticipation. I watch as she takes a sip, and her tongue darts out to lick her lips. She catches me staring, and a playful smirk graces her lips as she asks, eyes hooded with desire, "Want a taste?"

I hesitate. I know she's teasing me to see if I am attracted to her, too. I also know I shouldn't give in to what we both seem to want. My head is yelling at me to resist but the rest of me yells louder and so, I nod and lean in, closing the distance between us.

"You sure you're ready for it?" she asks, voice breathy. She takes another sip and runs her tongue over her lips.

A shiver runs down my spine at the sight, knowing I can't wait any longer. I take the glass from her hand, set it aside, and pull her close again. As our lips meet, I can taste the wine and feel the hint of danger and desire sparking in the air.

"That's delicious," I murmur, feeling a warmth spread through me that has nothing to do with the wine.

Emma's eyes sparkle with amusement as she smiles coyly. "I'm glad you like it," she says, taking another sip and softly sighing. "It is a secret recipe."

Before I can ask her more about the secret, Emma leans in again, boldly, her lips hovering just inches from mine.

"You know, there's something else I want to taste," she whispers, her voice low and sultry.

My heart clenches as I realize what she's hinting at. I lean in slowly, our lips meeting in a fiery, passionate kiss. She licks my bottom lip with the tip of her tongue, pulling it into her mouth, teasing me. She slowly moves her hand from my shoulder to my chest, sliding up my shirt until she reaches my chin.

Her fingers are cool against my hot skin. The sensation of her touch sends electric shocks through my body, making me crazy with want of her. I smell her jasmine perfume, and it makes me feel slightly dizzy. We've both been working so hard this week. We deserve a little break.

Our connection seems so real, more real than anything I've felt before. Days of wanting her make this moment too good to be true. My mind begins to wander. I'm no longer just some guy sitting in his bedroom fantasizing about this beautiful woman. Here she is right before me, kissing me passionately. Is it really possible?

Her lips part, allowing her breath to tickle the inside of my earlobe. She smiles, and then she starts moving again, taking my hands and putting them around her waist. Our bodies press together closely, and I feel every curve under her clothes. I pull her closer, relishing the feeling of her breasts pressing against my chest. I put my arms around her shoulders, and she gently pushes them down, letting me hold her close.

Then she moves away, leaving me breathless and wanting more. With a wicked smile, she slowly pulls her shirt off, and then her pants, leaving little to my imagination. Her hands pull at my clothes, her intentions clear. She takes those toned legs and straddles my lap. I kiss her neck as she slowly raises herself, sitting on my thighs. The kiss is slow and tender, her breath hot against my cheek when she finally breaks away. I reach behind her back and unclasp her bra. I run my fingers over the soft skin of her breasts, and she moans softly.

"Mmm... that feels nice," she purrs, kissing me again. She continues to kiss me and rub her breasts against my chest. I pull her close, rubbing her back with one hand while running my other hand between her legs under her barely-there lacy thong. Her hips buck against my palm. She smiles seductively, leaning forward to kiss me. She teases me for a few minutes, not breaking the kiss long enough to let me touch her breasts or pussy. When I finally do, she grabs my wrist and pulls my hand to her nipple instead. I suck on her nipple, giving it a gentle tug, eliciting another moan from her.

"Ooh... take me now," she whispers, straddling my thigh. "Please."

She rubs herself against my hard cock, causing it to throb. She gives it a few quick strokes before holding it firmly and then lowers herself down on it. I can't help but thrust upwards, trying to move deeper into her. But she holds onto my shoulders tightly, preventing me from pushing in any further.

"Oh God, that feels good," she says softly. "Slowly now..." She rocks her hips back and forth, teasing me. Her breathing is heavy, and her chest rises and falls rapidly as she holds my gaze.

"Are you sure you can handle it?"

"I'm ready, just do not stop... please," she says and then begins to rock faster, riding me for all she's worth. She slows down for a second and then resumes her pace. I grab her boobs and caress them, rolling her erect nubs between my fingers, causing her to moan loudly. She breathes hard, her eyes closed, and her lips parted. She looks so sexy sitting on my lap, grinding her pussy against my cock, writhing from the pleasure.

The sight of her naked body and the feelings she's causing in me makes it impossible to hold back. After a few minutes, I know I won't last much longer. "Oh god... I'm going to cum," I groan.

With that, I lose control, grunting wildly as my orgasm rushes through my body. I throw my head back, moaning loudly as I cum so hard I see stars. She collapses on my lap, gasping and panting. I hold her tight, gently stroking her back.

"Well, I guess we do not need that rollaway bed, now..." I chuckle, all thoughts of the competition beyond the four walls of our room long forgotten.

Emma looks up at me with a mischievous grin on her face. "I guess not," she replies, still panting. "But we might need some towels."

CHAPTER 4

Stuck Together

EMMA

The snow begins to fall harder, and the city is changed instantly. I never knew that I would share a hotel room with Max, but I am sharing, and now it seems like this hotel room is going to be our home for a very long time. The easy charm of Denver is now shrouded in a veil of white, as if the sky has opened up and released a storm of delicate white cotton on it. It looks beautiful, but as it intensifies, I also feel a sense of fear. Late spring storms in the area can become violent, I've been told. The cold breezes hit me like a punch in the face, making me shiver as soon as I open the window.

"This was a bad idea," I say to myself.

"It sure was, Emma." Max's voice comes from behind as he wakes up slowly.

I immediately close the window, and Max approaches me, taking me in his arms as I shiver. I glance outside, looking at the thick and heavy snowflakes falling from the sky with a vengeance, each unique in its own way.

"Let's go outside," I say to Max. "We have to wait for the camera crew to show up and I doubt that will happen anytime soon. So, let's take advantage of our delayed start time today!" I love snow, and this unexpected snowfall urges me to enjoy it fully.

"Do I have a choice, Emma?" Max asks sarcastically.

"It looks like... no!" I reply with a smile as I grab his arm dragging him away from the window.

I stand outside in the snow-covered terrace of our hotel as I feel the soft, cold flakes fall onto my face. I shield my eyes, taking in the beauty of this winter wonderland created by nature. I roam around like a kid getting excited about the snowfall, and Max glances at me with amusement every now and then. My shoes crunch against the snow beneath them as I admire the spectacular contrast of white snow and the darkening sky.

"You really like snow, Emma," Max says to me.

"Yes, I love it," I say as my breath comes out in a puff of white as I spin around, taking Max's hand in my hand as the snowflakes continue to fall around us. The city's busy streets are now quiet and still, with only a few people venturing out. The lights are muted, and glittering buildings are hidden under the vast blanket of snow.

I can't resist the urge to scoop soft, white snow from the floor and pack it into a tight ball as I throw it with a grin toward Max.

"Watch it," I say, chuckling as my snowball hits him in the back with a gentle thud.

I laugh out loud as we start playing together, feeling playfulness and childlike wonder that we have almost forgotten exists.

Soon, the sounds of the wind quickly escalate into the beginning of a storm and becomes deafening, like a chorus.

"Emma, we should go inside," Max says. We walk through the snow, but every step is heavy and laborious. The wind around us seems to slow down, as we can see no one around. The chuckling and sweet laughter of children playing in the snow has subsided. Life is on pause as I cling to Max's jacket as we walk toward our hotel's lobby.

"I have never seen Denver this quiet and serene," Max says as I nod. The heavy wind with thick snowflakes starts to push against us like an invisible force. We finally make it back to our hotel room, but we are soaked to the bone and frozen to the core. I can't wait to warm up with a hot cup of cocoa and snuggle up in a blanket with Max.

As we both remove our wet clothes and put on dry ones, huddling together, we hear a knock on our door. Max answers it, only to find the hotel manager standing outside, looking frazzled and out of breath.

"What happened?" Max asks.

"Excuse me, sir. I'm sorry to disturb you, but I have some bad news," the manager says tensely.

"What's going on?" I ask, coming towards the door, as I can easily sense something is wrong.

"There's a snowstorm outside," the manager replies.

"Yeah, so?" I ask.

"It is severe, and we've been advised by the local authorities to tell our guests to stay indoors until the storm passes. I'm afraid you won't be able to resume your competition until tomorrow at the earliest," he says. "Electrical surges can be dangerous, and we can't risk having a dozen ovens going at once."

"What?" Max says with disbelief in his voice.

"Are we stuck here?" I ask.

"I'm afraid so," the manager says.

"I'm so sorry for the inconvenience, but it is for your safety," he adds as I look out at the window, everything so quickly covered in the thick layer of white snow.

"What are we supposed to do?" I ask with a note of panic in my voice.

"We will try to arrange something as soon as possible," he says.

"Until then, we have a fully stocked bar and restaurant in the hotel. And there's a game room with a pool table and other amenities. You could make yourselves comfortable and ride out the storm here," he adds.

Max sighs, running his hand through his hair.

"Fine, I guess we do not have a choice," he says, surrendering to the situation.

"I'm sorry again for the inconvenience. We'll do everything possible to make your stay comfortable," the manager says before leaving us puzzled and unsure what to do next.

"Well, I guess we should make the best of it," I say, trying to lift our moods.

"Yeah, I suppose. I can't believe we're stuck here," he says, still with a hint of frustration and anger.

"I know, but what can we do about it?" I say, trying to reason with him.

"I don't know, but I just feel trapped," Max says, pacing back and forth.

"Maybe we should just try to get some rest. We'll be able to leave in the morning," I say, and he nods back, but I can still see him worried about what will happen.

"This is insane. I've never seen snow like this," he says.

"I know, right?" I reply. "You know what? Let's make the best of this situation. Let's have a snowball fight!" I add.

"Not now, Emma. Are you serious? We're stuck inside!" he says, ignoring the sarcasm.

Suddenly, there is a knock on the door again, and I open it to find a hotel employee standing outside with a tray.

"Excuse me. We're offering all our guests free hot drinks and snacks due to the inconvenience caused."

"I could use some hot cocoa right about now," I say as he places the tray with hot cocoa and some snacks on the table.

"You know, Max, this snowstorm might have ruined our plans, but I'm glad we got stuck together," I say as we both sip from our respective mugs, looking at each other with admiration and passion.

Sitting on the comfortable couch, I lean over to Max, pressing our bodies together, our lips meeting in a passionate kiss. The warmth of Max's breath mingles in the air as our tongues dance in each other's mouths in a heated embrace. I run my fingers through his hair, pulling him closer as he roams his hand on my back, tracing my curves. Every touch and caress sends a jolt of electricity running through my body as I lose myself in Max's embrace. His lips are soft and gentle against my skin, creating a hunger in our kiss as he nips at my lower lip, teasing me with his tongue before plunging back for another deep, sensual kiss. I moan in his mouth as my body comes alive with desire.

I have never felt like this before, and now I can only think about Max, his touch, his scent, his taste. I have never wanted someone this much, never felt so alive with the rush of desire as our lips part. I can feel his tongue sweeping into my mouth, with our bodies so close. Max's hands trail down my back to my hips before settling on my thighs. He lifts me up, pulling me onto his lap so that I am straddling him. I grind my hips against him, feeling the heat between us. His hands are everywhere on my body, stroking my breasts underneath my shirt and then teasing my nipples. I arch my back riding the waves of pleasure as the kiss intensifies until it feels like I am on the brink of explosion. As I look into his eyes, I break away from Max's lips, gasping for air.

"Take me, Max," I whisper. "Take me now," I say as he stands up, wrapping his arms tightly around me and carrying me towards the bed, tossing me onto it like I'm a feather.

The heat of our passion is burning like wildfire, and our bodies are intertwined. He places his lips onto mine as we savor the taste of each other. But as quickly as this kiss started, it ended as he pulled away, breaking the embrace and standing up abruptly. He leaves me sitting on the couch, my heart pounding and my body trembling with desire. He turns away, breathing heavily as he tries to regain control.

"Max, what's wrong?" I ask as I see conflict in his eyes.

"I can't do this, Emma. We can't keep doing this," Max says in a strained voice, and I feel my heart sinks as the reality of this situation comes crashing down on me.

"But Max, we have something special," I say, standing up and reaching out to him. "We can't just ignore our feelings." I add.

"I know, Emma. Believe me, I know how much I want this. But if we continue down this path, it will only end in heartbreak," he says as tears start to well up in my eyes.

"Emma, don't cry, please. I don't want that," he says as I turn back, lying on the bed, curling up. But Max comes back, hugging me from behind, and his cock touches my back.

"Do you really want it, Emma? Are you ready for it?" Max asks me.

"Not when you don't want it," I reply, maintaining my curled-up position.

"Emma, I want it. I am just afraid about the future," he replies as he turns me around so I can face him. "We've been thrown together unexpectedly and now the competition has been shut down due to the storm. But the storm won't last forever. Don't we need to think about tomorrow? Eventually, if we keep winning in our brackets, we'll have to compete directly against each other. Then what?"

"Do you really feel like thinking about the future right now?" I ask.

"Not really," Max replies as he gently kisses my lips again and unzips his pants.

"You snapped out of professional mode fast," I say with a smile while Max undresses me completely, and I stand naked in front of him. He locks his eyes on my body.

"What are you seeing?" I ask.

"You, your beautiful body," he says as he grabs me by my waist, pulling me closer as he pushes us both onto the soft mattress. His cock slaps against the flesh of my skin, radiating burning heat from our bodies.

"Max, I really need you inside me," I repeat my words again as he touches my glistening center with his dick, sending a shiver down my spine. His touch is turning me on more, and the sounds of the snowstorm outside, add more passion to the energy of the room. Max starts to thrust inside my pussy, and I pull him close, creating a trail of kisses on his neck.

"I am enjoying you even more than I imagined," Max says.

"I said so," I reply as we both are lost in our fantasy world, where nothing else matters to me except for Max and giving in to our desires. Max starts to stroke back and forth, maintaining a tight grip on my hips. We both come close to orgasm as he thrusts in again for the last time, pulling his dick out as his hot liquid erupts from his cock, wetting my belly. We both lay tangled in each other's arms, feeling the intensity of our lovemaking. The sheets on the bed are rumpled around us as evidence of our passion. I nestle my head in his chest and listen to the steady pounding rhythm of his heartbeat. I wrap my arms around him as I feel the same wall coming up between us again.

"Is everything okay?" I ask softly, and he nods, an awkward silence between us. The weight of our unspoken feelings hang heavy in the air. I know this night has changed everything, but

I can't force him into anything he isn't ready for. I know he's worried about the competition. He was so thoroughly in the zone before we first hooked up, and now I think he's afraid he can't get his mind back to that single-minded focus again. For whatever reason, I don't feel the same. I know I can snap right back to work when the time comes. Can't I? Or am I just lying to myself.

CHAPTER 5

The Morning After

MAX

I wake up in bed and look to my other side. The pillow is empty and cold, and Emma is gone. I let out a deep sigh.

What is happening, I wonder. I am curious to know how things turned out this way.

Everything was going well. Emma and I were in a competition together, and we did what all our rivals did, we were competing against each other.

Then suddenly, I was feeling drawn towards her. I felt something that I have never felt before in my life, and then, before you knew it, we were making out. One thing led to another with us, and we ended up sleeping together again.

I am not saying I don't like her. I think I might like her a bit too much, and I do not know what to do about it. I do not know if I should go talk to her about it or leave things as they are.

I really want to tell her how I feel, though. I want her to know that I want to be with her. I just don't know if either of us are ready for any dating labels, yet. I want to get to know her better, and I want her to get to know me.

Instead of being rivals in a competition, we can be with each other as partners and extend our bond beyond this one competition. Winning is losing is allure for me as my heart is awakening to the feelings I have when I'm around her. Her sassy attitude drew me in and now her softer side is keeping me captive.

But I do not know whether I should talk to her about it. I do not want to make things awkward between us, and I definitely do not want to lose whatever this is that we have right now.

Since we spend so much time together, things can get weird if I tell her I have feelings for her.

I enter the shower so I can think better. A hot shower always helps me clear my mind.

What if she doesn't have feelings for me? What if this is just a fling for her, and she doesn't want to make it more serious? I can't do that. I think and think as I let the water from the shower calm me down.

But what if she feels the same way. What if by keeping my feelings to myself, I am actually ruining stuff for us. Maybe she is waiting for me to tell her how I feel, and then she will reciprocate that? I mean, girls usually wait for guys to make the first move, so who knows, she might actually be into me but isn't doing anything because I haven't done anything, either. I start thinking positively.

My mind is running, and I can't stop thinking about all the "What ifs" and "Maybes" of my situation with Emma.

I need to deal with this. It is very distracting for me. And since I am in a baking competition and I came here to win, I can't let anything distract me, not even Emma.

I steel my resolve. I am not going to let anything get in the way of me and winning this competition. I came here to win, and that is precisely what I am going to do. I do not want to be distracted with love and all the other feelings that come along with it. I want to prove that I am a chef.

I get out of the shower as my mind is making me understand that I am not interested in love and relationships and that I am only here for the competition, but deep down, I know that this is all a lie. I want to talk to Emma, and I do not know what I will do if I do not get to express my feelings to her.

I make myself a coffee from the little pot in the room and get ready to go out, as today is our day off from the competition. The next round takes place tomorrow. I know that I can't let my personal feelings get in the way of this competition, and one thing I know about Emma is that she is definitely not going to back down just because of her personal feelings. So, I should do the same.

I get dressed and grab my phone. I see a text from Emma.

"Sorry I left without telling you, we have the next round tomorrow, and I need to prepare for that." Her text is straight to the point.

As expected, unlike me, Emma didn't let her feelings get in the way of her work. She is busy preparing for the next round while I am here, stuck thinking about how beautiful her smile is. I mean, to be fair, she has the most gorgeous smile that I have ever seen.

When she smiles, I feel like my whole world lights up. I can feel my heart beating faster when she looks at me as she smiles. And her laugh... oh God, her laugh is like music to my ears. Every time she lets out a loud laugh with her hand covering her mouth and her eyes sparkling, I feel like I am falling for her over and over again.

I love when she tucks her curly hair behind her ear because it is getting in the way of her cooking, and how she frowns in a cute way when she can't get something done the right way. I love every little detail about her.

"Get a hold of yourself, Max," I say out loud to myself as I find myself thinking about her again while staring at the text from her.

"Hey, no, it is all cool," I type, but I do not send. I think a million times before I send the text. I type and erase and then type again. Finally, I send it to her. She doesn't respond right away. I keep checking my phone, but there's nothing.

I look at my small hotel room coffee and feel like I need something stronger to start my day. I bundle up the best I can and head outside the hotel to the coffee shop across the street to get myself an Americano. Only an Americano can distract me from all these thoughts.

I wait in the line, forcing my brain to focus on the recipe I have planned for tomorrow's bake off. We are nearing the final rounds and I don't want to be eliminated.

"One Americano, please," I hear the person ahead of me order, and it hits me. I know that voice. All my resolve melts away. It is her. Emma. I would recognize that voice anywhere. Her sweet, honey-like tone is special, just like she is. I can't help but smile as I think about the surprise of seeing her here, both of us fueling up before we get back to the business of baking.

Emma turns around and sees me looking at her. She immediately gasps, and then a beautiful smile shows up across her face.

"Great minds, huh?" she asks me, raising her hot coffee in her hand.

"We better not have the same grand finale recipe planned this weekend," I tease, trying to keep the conversation where it needs to be: professional.

"Do you want to wait for me a minute and have our coffee together?" I slip out the question casually, the emotional part of me winning for the moment.

"Sure, not as a date, though," Emma blurts out in her charming way and laughs. "Oh, I can't believe I just said that out loud!"

Something in her eyes lets me know she meant every word. I feel a little deflated.

"No, no, hahaha, just saying that because we are both in the shop getting the same coffee, so how about we hang out for a while," I say, trying to make myself clear.

"Oh yeah, of course," she says as she tries to not make eye contact with me. I can't believe this conversation just happened. "I can update you on the status of the show, anyway. I went down to the kitchens earlier. Everyone is antsy because of the delay."

I order my coffee to go, and then we head out.

"So, you are an Americano fan, too, huh?" she asks me, breaking the silence.

"Oh, always, you will always find me drinking this in the morning," I say.

"I think it is the best thing to-" I start to say.

"Wake me up in the morning," we both say at the same time, and then we look at each other and laugh.

"Are you excited for the next round tomorrow?" Emma asks me.

"Yes, I can't wait to beat you," I say as I smirk.

"Huh, beat me? You wish," Emma scoffs, and I laugh. I'm glad to have our old banter back. She looks at me, rolls her eyes, and then laughs. I love her beautiful smile.

"You have a lovely smile," I say to her. I know that I decided to keep my personal feelings aside, but I just can't help myself when I am in front of her. Whenever I am with her, I just want to grab her and kiss her passionately.

"Thank you," Emma says shyly.

She looks at me, and our eyes meet each other's, but we do not say anything.

I keep looking at her, my eyes staring at her lips and then back at her eyes. I move in closer to her, as if drawn in by an invisible force.

She comes closer to me. I can feel her breath on me, and it is driving me insane. I cannot help but stare down at her body. Even all bundled up, she is so sexy, has curves in all the right places, and her beauty is undeniable. As she is coming closer to me, I cannot deny what I am feeling right now. *How am I going to resist this girl?*

I keep staring at her lips, and our eyes meet for a moment. I get that she knows what I am thinking, and she is thinking the same thing. She comes closer to me, her eyes going from looking at my lips to staring at my eyes. I know for sure now that I am going to kiss this girl.

I look at her one more time before I give in, put my arm around her, and pull her in for a kiss.

I place my hand on her back and bring her even closer to me, her breath softly hitting me. *I need her so badly.* I press my lips on hers. Every other thing intensifies as our lips crush together and we taste each other. It feels like this is the end of the world. The world comes to a halt as our tongues roll with each other.

Knowing that we both can't resist each other anymore makes me feel even more excited about this. I grab her even more tightly, her tongue inside my mouth, tasting me, her hands behind my neck and gently running through my hair, my hands holding her tightly from the back.

I gently push her back to the wall. We stand just outside the hotel, but no one is around and, even if they were, I don't care who sees. Now, I am in control of this kiss and giving it my all. My hands are restless, and I just want to take off her clothes right now. We go on kissing passionately before we break it off. We are both breathless and still holding each other close. She is staring at me while catching her breath, and I am looking at her, thinking about how lucky I am to be sharing this moment with her.

"That was..." I say as I catch my breath.

"Really hot," Emma completes my sentence.

She smiles, and I smile as I kiss her gently one more time.

I hold her hand in mine, and our fingers intertwine. I want to say it. I want to tell her right now how I feel about her. I want her to know that she is all I think about.

I take a deep sigh as I look at her one more time and kiss her again softly. I squeeze her hand, and she looks at me,

"Emma, I-" Before I could say anything, her phone rings.

Emma looks at her phone and then looks at me. I know she doesn't want to leave, either, but she has to, now.

"I have to go, Max," she says to me as she touches my face softly. Her fingers trace across my face. I kiss her hand. I hate to see her leave. I want to tell her how I feel.

"Maybe I will see you tonight?" I ask her, hoping that she says yes.

"We have the competition tomorrow, Max. I think we both know we can't hang out the night before the competition. I don't want to lose," she says to me as she smiles. I know that she can see the regret in my eyes, and I can see it in her eyes, too, though she is trying not to make it so obvious.

"Oh yeah. Definitely can understand that," I say, pretending to be cool.

"I will see you tomorrow, then." I wave her goodbye as she walks away while still looking at me.

"See you tomorrow, Max." She smiles, and I smile back at her. At this moment, it feels like I have fallen in love.

CHAPTER 6

Kitchen Showdown

EMMA

I wake up to the annoying sound of my alarm. I groan into the pillow.

"Turn it off," I mumble as I bury my face in the pillow, trying to escape the shrill sound of the alarm, but it never stops.

I open my eyes and turn to see the time, only to find that it is six a.m.

I sit up instantly as everything comes back to me. The competition! I have to be there at eight a.m. My god, how could I be so careless?

I stumble out of my bed and rush to the bathroom where I quickly brush my teeth and take a shower. I'm back in my old room with the plumbing thankfully working exactly as it should this time.

I only have ten minutes to get ready. I contemplate between either blow-drying my hair or just pulling it up in a tight bun as it is.

"Fuck it. It has to be tied up, anyway," I say to myself as I quickly dry my hair with a towel and pull it into a tight bun, making sure not a single hair is out of place.

Fire and Flame is one of the most prestigious cooking competitions in the world for a reason. They demand the best of the best, and even that isn't enough. I have seen that firsthand with the kind of struggles other chefs have faced the past week. And they have very strict rules about their dress code. If any hair is found in a dish, it calls for instant elimination, and I am not going to risk this at any cost.

As soon as I am dressed in my chef's uniform, along with my hair net, I step outside and rush towards the kitchen that I will be using. Even as I walk towards it, I feel myself getting more and more nervous. Could I do this? If my dad, someone who is obviously a way better chef than me, could not win, what were the odds that I could take this trophy home?

Not to mention that the other competitors in this competition are way more experienced than I am. Thinking of other competitors instantly reminds me of Max.

Not that I have been able to forget him at all. Somehow, Max has found a way to infiltrate my every thought ever since the day we met. The first time I met him, my body reacted to him in a way that it had never reacted to anyone else. No matter how much I tried, I could not deny the attraction I felt towards him.

I know I should stay away from him and that I am only complicating things for myself and him by continuing this thing between us. But it doesn't matter how much I try to make myself understand. Every time I see him, I feel this intense need to be in his arms, to press my lips to his, and to let his tongue consume my mouth. Kissing him has quickly become my favorite thing to do. I love how he kisses me, softly at first but never lacking the hunger and passion that we both feel toward each other.

Even though he tried to put a stop to this and tried to tell me that this was only going to complicate things for us in the future, I didn't listen to him. The truth is that I haven't felt this way for anyone in so long, and now that I have, I do not want to let it go. The consequences be damned.

The first time Max kissed me, I knew I was a goner. Something about the way his arms wrapped around me and how his lips descended on me had me addicted. I threw caution out the window right then and there. And before I knew it, Max and I were in bed, with him hovering over me as he continued to make love to me. I could not say I regretted it because I didn't.

But I am conflicted. It is no secret that whatever Max and I have has to be temporary. But somehow, I am drawn to him more than just in a physical way. I have found a friend in Max, despite the fact that he is my competitor. The way he teases me, makes me laugh, and most importantly, the way he understands me has all been messing with my head. I have started to like him more than just as someone I like to hook up with. I like him for who he is, and that thought makes me worried, knowing that

I am only signing myself up for heartbreak if I keep letting this thing escalate.

I am curious to know if whatever I am feeling is even reciprocated by Max. He has never said anything, nor has he indicated in any way that he wants anything more than a physical relationship, and I fear that if I do not tamper down my own emotions, I will be the only one who suffers in the end. Not to mention that developing feelings for someone who is a competitor will only distract me from my goal, and I could not let that happen. Nothing is more important to me than winning this competition and proving myself to my father.

As soon as I reach the kitchen, I brush all the thoughts of Max aside and say, "I can't let my attention wander at any cost. I am here for a reason, and nothing will stop me or get in the way of my goals."

I enter the massive kitchen, which stretches over a thousand square feet and has an airy atmosphere due to the high ceilings, giving the numerous contestants space to breathe freely no matter how many people are scattered around the kitchen. There are several shiny counters for each contestant, lined with stainless steel appliances for use. The room is brightened with a combination of natural light streaming in from large windows and bright artificial lights.

My eyes move to the pantry area in the kitchen, stocked with every ingredient imaginable. It has every spice, herb, vegetable, fruit, and pasta known to humans sitting there, waiting to be picked up and converted into a delicious meal.

On the other side of the kitchen, a whole area has been designated for the purpose of plating and presentation to avoid any kind of hassle.

Fire and Flame is a competition that has been taking place for years now, and it shows. The kitchen set-up is designed for efficiency and practicality while also being luxurious, with high-end finishes and top-of-the-line equipment. This is the kind of kitchen I saw on television as a kid when I used to be obsessed with cooking shows. This is the kind of kitchen that any chef would salivate over, and it is the perfect space for a cooking competition as large as this one.

As my eyes travel over the whole expanse of the kitchen, taking in every detail, they clash with gray, smoldering eyes that seem to be already looking my way. My heartbeat quickens as I pause my inspection of the kitchen, and my eyes rake over Max. He somehow manages to look just as handsome in a white apron as he does in his casual clothing. Even the hair net on his head doesn't make him look silly like it does with me, which makes me huff. My breath hitches as I notice Max's lips lift into an amused smile as he looks at me.

God, he looks so good when he smiles. I think dreamily.

Snap out of it! I scold myself as I walk toward him. As soon as I reach him, I hear his teasing words.

"I thought you had chickened out, not that I can blame you. Who wouldn't when I am their competitor?" he says in a smug voice that makes me roll my eyes even as a contagious smile makes its way to my face.

"I would much rather throw myself from this building's roof than give up and let you win," I scoff dramatically as I sit down next to him on the seats placed on one side of the room.

"Then, maybe you should rethink the implications of that statement, Emma, because I am going to win this competition," he says with a smirk.

"We'll see about that," I say with the same amount of confidence.

Our stare-off is interrupted by the sound of a throat clearing. I quickly turn around to see one of our judges, a very famous and well-known chef from France, George, standing up and bringing everyone's attention to himself.

"First of all, I want to welcome you all to the Fire and Flame competition. I doubt I have to say much about how big of a deal it is that you all have made it this far into the competition and have a chance to stand here today and compete against each other. Only a select few people get the opportunity to stand in this kitchen and compete to win this competition, so before we even begin, I want you all to acknowledge this victory for yourself. No matter who wins today, always remember that you still made it here, and then try again until you win." He says it in a loud and clear voice.

His words give me confidence. He is right. I have achieved what so few are able to achieve, and no matter what happens today, I won't lose hope. We started out with over twenty contestants last week and now, there are just a few of us remaining. This part of the show is televised so the pressure is immense.

"And if that isn't enough to make you feel better, let me tell you that you are one of the luckiest people in this competition since today, instead of deciding on the type of dessert ourselves, we have decided to let you choose whatever you want to bake. Whatever you think is your best dessert, regardless of its ingredients, you can make it. You have one hour and forty-five minutes to present us with your best dessert. Good luck!" he announces before returning to his place next to the other judges.

I share a surprised look with Max as we both digest this news. This is the first time this has happened. One of the reasons why this is one of the most challenging competitions to win is because of the tricky dishes the judges choose, but today is a good day for us.

As soon as the 15 minutes for us to get everything from the pantry and refrigerators start, I rush to grab a basket, and as soon as I reach the section for baking, I instantly decide what I am going to make.

I quickly pick up two boxes of flour and sugar, along with everything else I need for the same cupcakes that my father had made when he participated in this competition. If I am going to win this, I will win it by making the exact same recipe he made when he participated. This is my form of revenge.

As I collect things for my vanilla cupcakes and the salted caramel filling, I intend to add them in when my eyes fall over to Max piling his basket with cream cheese, graham crackers, peaches, and oranges, and I instantly figure out his dish. His peach, orange cheesecake is a very famous dessert that everyone has heard of, and people travel miles just to taste it. My nervousness only increases with the knowledge, and I think of how I could win with my salted caramel cupcakes when he is making his world-famous cheesecake.

As soon as I get to my spot, I lose myself in the process of mixing my ingredients, letting the world fade away as I focus all my attention on making sure everything is perfect. When I finally place my cupcakes in the oven, fifteen minutes have already passed. I instantly start working on my salted caramel filling, tuning out the clangs of movement and actions of the other contestants.

When I am done with my filling, I finally look up and see that only forty-five minutes are left before the timer goes off. The heat in the kitchen increases as the competition intensifies, with everyone determined to win. My eyes drift to where Max is whisking the gelatin into his peach-orange jelly. I can't help but stare as his biceps flex as he whisks away, swooning from inside. No matter how much I try, I can't help but be distracted by my feelings for Max, but I manage to brush everything away and focus on my caramel buttercream.

When only fifteen minutes are left, I start filling the cupcakes with the salted caramel filling I have prepared and rush to the area for plating as I carefully assemble my cupcakes on the plate, pipe the Caramel Swiss Buttercream on top of the cupcakes, and sprinkle them with pecan coconut brittle crumble. As soon as I am done, the judges announce that the time is over, and we proceed to the waiting area.

We make small talk with the other contestants until we are called back by the judges for the announcement.

"We want you all to know that we have had the chance to taste some of the best desserts today, but sadly, only one could be the winner. If I am going to be honest, we were stuck between two amazing desserts, and the decision was really tough. But in the end, we decided that one of those dishes deserved to win. So, the winner of this year's Fire and Flame is... Emma Castello!" George declares.

My eyes widen with shock. Oh my god, I can't believe it! I have done it! I won! In my excitement, I turn towards Max, and without even thinking, I jump into his arms, hugging him in excitement.

"Oh my god! Max, I did it. Can you believe it?" I squeal into his ears.

As soon as we pull back, unable to control myself, I press my lips to his and kiss him deeply. I feel his shock as he takes a moment to respond to my kiss until he wraps an arm around me and kisses me back with the same fervor.

This is definitely the best day of my life.

After Hours

MAX

I watch as Emma excitedly accepts everyone's congratulations and handshakes as she walks up to the judges to receive her medal and the prize money promised to her. Any other person in my place would be angry and bitter right now because someone else just won something they wanted to win really badly. And yes, I am a little disappointed that I did not win, but the truth is that seeing Emma this happy makes me feel content, as if her happiness is all that really matters anymore. When she jumped and hugged me the moment she won, I forgot that she was my competitor and that she had just won a competition I had worked hard to win. The only thing I could think of was how happy she looked, and nothing else mattered.

I still want to fulfill my mother's dream, and I will. But this time around, Emma won fairly, and she deserves this. I will try again and win for my mother, but for now, I will celebrate with Emma because of her success. Even though she has not told me her real reason for being here or the real reason for her interest in baking, I still do not care. All I care about is that she is happy, and I would do anything to make sure she keeps smiling this way.

When she is done greeting and sharing pleasantries with everyone, she returns to me, and I give her a big smile, my eyes shining with pride. No matter what, I am proud of her, and I always will be.

"Hi, champion," I say teasingly as I wrap my arm around her and pull her close.

"I did warn you, I will win," she says with a smug look on her face, which makes me laugh out loud as I lean down to kiss her softly on the lips.

"What are you doing tonight?" I ask her.

She raises an eyebrow at me in confusion as she answers, "Am I supposed to be doing something tonight?"

"Yes, you have plans with me tonight, beautiful," I tell her with a shrug.

"And what plans are these, may I ask?" she asks suspiciously.

"There is an after-party being held at the rooftop of this hotel for the contestants. And since you are the star of the show, I think it would be rude if you didn't join all the other contestants," I say teasingly.

"Alright, alright, no need to butter me up. I'll come with you. Just tell me what time I have to be ready," she says as she is acting resigned.

"We'll both leave at 7 p.m. How does that sound?" I say, as she nods in approval.

A few hours later, I am standing in the corridor of the hotel as I wait for Emma to finally get ready and come out so we can leave for the party.

"Emma! We will be late. Hurry up." I knock on the door, asking her to hurry up.

When I finally hear the door open, I turn around, ready to complain about her making me wait, but my words get caught in my throat as I take in her appearance.

She is wearing a red cocktail dress that hugs her curves in all the right places, and a slit starts from her mid-thigh as the gown pools down on the floor, exposing her smooth tan legs. I can't even find words to express how hot she looks right now. I just stand there, staring at her like a creep, until a laugh escapes her.

"Are you going to keep standing there, opening and closing your mouth like a goldfish, or will you say something?" She mocks me as she laughs at my bewildered expression.

"Emma... You look beautiful. This dress is made for you," I finally say after what seems like ages.

"Why, thank you. You clean up good, too," she says with a wink before she links her arm with mine, and we finally leave for the party.

We mingle for a few hours, clinking glasses and discussing the best restaurants in Denver, until I finally retreat and go to the bar to get a refill. I stand near the bar and look at Emma, who is excusing herself from everyone else and going to stand in one corner.

I walk towards her, wrap my arms around her from behind, and lean down to whisper in her ear, "Tired?"

She jolts a little in surprise but leans into my arms as she realizes it is me.

"A little," she confesses as she turns in my arms and wraps her arms around my neck. Her chest presses against mine, and I am instantly hyperaware of all the places she is touching me.

"Do you want me to help you relax?" I whisper into her ear seductively to which she just nods.

I pull back, grab her hand, and pull her toward the secluded area I found earlier on the covered rooftop. It is a quiet corner, completely hidden from intrusive eyes as the darkness of the night shadows our presence.

I pull her close to me the moment we are out of everyone's sight and kiss her hard, unable to control myself any longer.

"I think we should head back to our room" I whisper against her lips, and she nods.

We pull away and try to look presentable and head back to the room, the sexual tension between us palpable as we make our way back, avoiding speaking to anyone.

The minute we enter the door, our lips are on each other's, and we make our way to the bed.

She is lying over me, giving a trail of kisses on my neck, as she takes charge this time.

"Emma, you are being naughty today," I say smiling.

"Do you mind it?" she asks, flexing her authority on me.

"No! How could I mind a gorgeous girl lying on me?" I say smirking. Emma continues to kiss me.

"Do you want me inside?" I ask directly.

"Yes!" she replies wantonly, and I don't waste a second before entering her already wet pussy grabbing her tightly from the back. I toss her around, coming over to her, kissing and making my way inside her.

"Do it faster, Max." Emma says and I follow her lead, thrusting my erect cock inside her. A loud moan escapes her mouth bringing a wide smile on my face as I can't help but be attracted to her. Her flowery notes of fragrance are meeting with my sweat even in the chill of the room, hinting towards our passionate sex. She is struggling to stop her orgasm and I love seeing her like that.

"Max..." she gasps.

"I know what you want to say. Hold it for just a little more," I say.

"I...." She starts to say something when I forcefully thrust my dick inside her pussy for the final time before an eruption of passion leaves our bodies. Emma lies there in my arms as we cuddle, being grateful for this time together.

My fingers brush through Emma's hair as she sleeps peacefully on my chest. I stare at her, and I can't help but lean down and drop a kiss on her forehead. I can no longer deny it. I am falling for Emma. As much as I wanted to not fall for her and only keep this relationship physical, I just could not.

Emma has found a way inside my heart, and with every passing day, she only embeds herself deeper into my life and my heart. But the harsh reality is that I can't let this happen. I can't fall for Emma. This would never work out. We both are here temporarily, and soon, we will head back to our own lives in two different cities.

I need to detach from her, or else I am going to end up hurting myself. But how can I do that when all I can think of anymore is her. Wow, this is a mess.

CHAPTER 8

A Night to Remember

EMMA

The morning sun is rising over the skyline of Denver, casting a beautiful golden glow over the city. It is nine a.m. when my eyes snap open, and the crisp air carrying the scent of freshly brewed coffee hits my nostrils.

I slowly look around the room, my mind still foggy with sleep. It takes me a good one minute to figure out who is lying beside me. I am not alone. It is Max who is lying next to me, peacefully breathing deep and even. As soon as I see him, a rush of conflicting emotions flood my mind.

Why is he here? I ask myself, still struggling to figure out the reality when my mind immediately reminds me of last night. On the one hand, I am happy that he is beside me.

After all, there is undoubtedly something unusual between us. We are not just competitors. We are more than that, and we both know that. But on the other hand, I can't help but feel a twinge of guilt and confusion over our complicated and messed up relationship. Our casual fling is getting out of hand, and it is not something I want at this point in my life.

I look at him, appreciating how his messy hair covers his face as his chest rises up and down with each breath.

Damn! Despite all my reservations, I can still feel a string of desire deep within me. Oh God! Help me! I say to myself.

I lie beside him, thinking about all the times we shared together, the laughter, the passion, and the moments of vulnerability. Everything. He has been there for me even when I didn't realize I actually needed him. Despite the intense competition, he never did anything to piss me off.

The morning light starts filtering through the windows, and I know it is time to make some decisions. I get up to take in the view. I should either take a chance and see where things go or push him away, risking losing him forever.

Lose him forever. My heart sinks at my last words.

I can't afford that. I can't leave Max like that. I stand there at the window, talking to myself. In the distance, the towering mountains stand like beacons.

Things can't go on like this. I have to be honest with Max and myself. I can't keep playing this game of Tom and Jerry, where we both push and pull away after a few days. I think to myself. The sun is shining bright, and the warm rays start to hit my skin.

I look down at the deserted streets, returning to life as I spot some occasional early morning jogger or a worker heading to their job.

I walk toward the bathroom, leaving Max sleeping in the bed. I am conflicted, but I do not want to tell Max. I twist the shower knob, and the warm water from the showerhead cascades down my naked body, washing away the remnants of last night's sleep. I stand there, letting the water run over me, lost in my thoughts.

Max. The guy lying in the bed right now is not leaving my mind. Max is undoubtedly one of the most important parts of my trip to Denver and this competition. Over this whole competition, our relationship has grown complicated, especially after our intense lovemaking every now and then. We didn't think about what would happen next. We were just giving in to what was happening in the present, but now a pang of slight guilt is taking over me.

Why did I let him enter my life so quickly that the thought of losing him hurts me? Why did we both cross the line? We were competitors, and we should have remained that. But, no! We took it a step ahead without planning about the future. I say to myself.

The steam from the shower fills the small bathroom, adding to the feeling of isolation I am feeling right now. But this is precisely what I wanted. I want some alone time.

I want to open up to Max, but I do not really feel like it is the right time. I think while turning off the shower knob and wrapping myself in a fluffy bathrobe, making my way back to the bedroom where Max is still sleeping. I watch him for a moment, looking at his innocent expression, and wonder if he is as confused and conflicted about our relationship or if it is just me.

I grab my phone, sitting on the couch nearby, scrolling through social media, trying to distract myself from the thoughts swirling around my head, but nothing is helping me forget this mess I am in.

I am afraid of losing Max, but I am also so scared of coming closer to him. I fear being hurt but know I can't escape my feelings forever. I remind myself to stand up from my position and get dressed.

I have to be brave. I can't keep running away. I am here to enjoy, and that's what I will do. I say with complete determination as I get dressed in my comfortable white top and jeans.

I sit on the couch, waiting for Max to wake up, thinking about what happens next for me, the new champion of Fire and Flame.

It is the last night of the competition, and I am determined to win and celebrate my victory. I say to myself, feeling my heart racing with excitement and anxiety as I replay the night's events.

Okay. Now I must focus only on the competition and winning the battle I am here for in Denver. I have to make myself proud, and for that, I have to beat Max. And I will. But our relationship? My mind keeps taking me back.

I can't keep doing this. I need to move on. I mutter to myself, running my fingers through my hair. But this sudden pang of sadness that it is the last night of competition, and I won't be there with Max anymore hurts me.

Stop it, Emma. This competition is supposed to be a happy moment. I made lots of memories, and I got Max.

Ahh! Max again! I scold myself.

I have to focus on the good things in my life. I say to myself as a sense of determination washes over me. I think about all the hard work I have put into this competition. I think about the other people, the friends I made along the way, and the camaraderie that has grown between us all as we work together. And then, I think about Max again, one more positive thing about this competition.

I must be happy, celebrate my victory, and not let our complicated relationship hold me back. I say to myself, standing up from the couch, feeling light and free.

Finally, I can see Max stirring awake in front of my eyes.

"Hey there, sleepyhead," I say with a smile hiding away all my hurt and confusion. He rubs his eyes, yawning and stretching his arms above his head.

"Morning, Emma," he replies.

"What time is it?" he asks again.

"Pretty late. It is around 11 a.m." I reply.

"I guess we must have been tired," Max says with a chuckle as he smooths his hair.

"So, what's on the agenda for today, champ?" Max asks, rubbing his eyes again.

"First, maybe grab some brunch or something?" I say.

"Sounds good to me," Max replies, swinging his legs over the side of the bed. "Let me shower, and we can head out."

I nod, watching him go into the bathroom. Having him here with me and sharing these intimate moments is nice. But we have to make a decision.

Max emerges from the bathroom, all dressed up and ready to go, and we make our way out of the hotel room to the hotel restaurant.

"So, how did you sleep?" I ask, breaking the silence between us.

"Like a baby. Your bed is more comfortable than mine at home," Max says with a grin, and we both laugh, feeling a rush of emotions.

We enter the restaurant, greeted by the delicious aroma of freshly brewed coffee. We both go to a booth in a corner and scan the menu.

"Everything looks so good," I say, my stomach growling with hunger. He nods in agreement with a smile on his face.

After a few minutes of deliberation, we finally settled on our orders. I choose a classic eggs benedict, while Max opts for a hearty breakfast burrito. While we wait for our food to arrive, we sip on our coffees, chatting casually. I can't help but feel a sense of comfort and ease around him as if we've known each other for a long time.

The food arrives in between our chats. The eggs benedict is perfectly poached, with a creamy hollandaise sauce that melts in my mouth. Max's breakfast burrito is stuffed with eggs, cheese, and savory sausage wrapped in a warm tortilla.

After sharing some happy moments, we both agreed to explore the city and take in the sights.

We finish our meal and make our way out of the hotel.

We explore the city, hand in hand, making our relationship even more complicated, before returning to our hotel to enjoy the last night of the competition.

***

We both step into the grand ballroom of the hotel and are immediately awestruck by the beauty of the space. The entire room is decorated in shades of gold and silver, with glittering chandeliers hanging from the ceiling and luxurious drapes adorning the walls. In the center of the room is a massive dance floor, polished to a high shine, and surrounded by elegant tables and chairs. I can see our fellow competitors dressed in their finest attire and sipping champagne as they wait for the celebration to begin. I can feel a sense of excitement rising within me as I realize, again, that I won this prestigious competition.

It is going to be an unforgettable night, I say to myself as I move to the beat of the music the band is playing, feeling a sense of joy coursing through my veins.

The hotel has outdone itself with the decorations and atmosphere, and I am grateful to be a part of it all.

"Let's celebrate," I say, taking Max's hand and pulling him towards the dance floor after we both greet all our fellow competitors. The music is loud and pulsing, and I feel lost in it. I spin around, lost in the music and the magic of the night, feeling a sense of euphoria washing over me.

This kind of celebration only occurs once in a lifetime, and I am determined to make the most of it. With each twirl, I can feel a unique connection building with Max.

I do not want this magical moment to end. I think to myself as a bittersweet sadness washes over me. Denver, this ballroom, and the dance have become a memory, a symbol of the celebration and the magic for me. I know this memory of winning the competition will last a lifetime. It is a reminder of the joy and celebration that will never be forgotten.

Max was a little hesitant at first, but my energy soon moved him to the rhythm as we clinked our wine glasses together.

"Cheers to Emma!" he says, bringing a wide smile to my face as I feel our closeness.

"You were amazing," Max says, admiring me.

"Thanks," I reply as I blush, feeling a surge of warmth in my chest as he leans close to me, and his hot breath touches my face.

I can feel the heat rising between us, and I know that I want to be with him, and without thinking, I lean in and kiss him, our lips meeting in a passionate rush. Our tongues continue to swirl inside each other's mouths, savoring the sweet taste of each other as we kiss for what feels like an eternity.

We pull away feeling breathless, as I feel a sense of joy and contentment washing over me. I have won the cooking competition but winning his heart is equally important.

CHAPTER 9

Last Chance

MAX

"What's next?" I ask Emma after we both danced our hearts out in the ballroom.

"Let's go out and get a little fresh air. We have a lot to celebrate," she replies with excitement evident in her voice.

"Sure," I say, nodding. "It's a lot warmer out than it was three days ago."

The chilly night air in Denver only adds to the celebration The crowd in and outside the hotel is thick, as friends and family of the competitors join together for the last evening's gala. Amidst the happy crowds, Emma and I walk hand in hand together.

"I can't believe how amazing the past week has been," Emma says, her voice filled with emotion.

"Yeah, it is pretty wild, isn't it?" I reply, chuckling and squeezing her hand.

I spot a small, graveled path leading off the main road into what looks like an alleyway. I can see buildings further down, including a few dive bars.

"Hey, let's check this out," I say, gesturing toward the darkened path.

"Sure, why not," Emma replies after a few seconds of hesitation. She follows me into the dimly lit alleyway. The narrow alleyway is lined with graffiti-covered walls. I grab her hand, pulling her towards a door on the side, and she follows me through the door, trusting me completely. The small, dimly lit bar is filled with thick air and smoke. The live music adds to the vibe as the band plays jazz, and the patrons sway along to the beat. We order a few drinks, settle into a booth in the corner of the room, sip on our drinks, and listen to the music as we watch the dancers twirl around the small dance floor.

"Emma," I call to her.

"What, Max?" she replies.

"I wanted to win this competition and never expected to lose. But you won it. And it brings equal happiness to me," I confess.

"Any of us could have won it," she replies graciously.

"But you were exceptional," I say.

"You were not too bad yourself," she replies, giggling.

"I know. I am a force to be reckoned with," I reply, keeping the sarcasm intact.

"Ah...Yes! I saw it in our initial meetings," she replies.

"I can't imagine it would all be so different in just a few meetings. Although we started off on the wrong foot, it is nothing like that now," I say.

"Yeah." She nods, cutting off the topic.

"This is amazing. I can't believe we stumbled upon this place," she says.

"That's the beauty of Denver. You never know what you're going to find," I reply.

The night wears on, and we continue exploring the city, wandering through the streets and discovering hidden gems. We stop at a food truck, share a plate of spicy tacos, and make our way to the rooftop cafe to take in the stunning views of the city.

"This has been the most incredible night," she says, her eyes shining in the moonlight.

"I'm glad we could experience it together," I reply softly, entwining my fingers with hers.

It is our last night, a last chance to be together, and I do not want this to end so soon. I want to tell Emma that I am taking her heart back home. I must tell her I love her, but I just can't. The fear of losing her is more than my courage.

We sit silently for a few minutes, lost in our thoughts.

"I do not want this night to end," Emma interrupts, her voice filled with longing.

"Me either," I reply, causing an awkward silence between us again.

I can feel that we both are on the same page, but neither of us dares to confess our feelings.

I know that we both feel the same way. Her touch and face tell me she is also in love with me. But what if she isn't? What if I am picking up all the wrong signals? I tell myself before we set off again.

We walk silently for a few moments. The only sound is the soft click of our footsteps on the pavement.

"I have something to show you," I say with a hint of excitement. I come across this place from an Instagram influencer, and I really want to explore this place. But exploring it with Emma makes it even more memorable for me. She looks at me curiously, wondering what I will show her. I lead her back toward the hotel, the sound of running water growing louder as we get closer. At the end of the small path, we find a small fountain and the water glistening in the moonlight.

"It is beautiful," Emma says as we gaze at it intensely.

I reach into my pocket and pull out a small box, opening it to reveal a delicate necklace.

"And I wanted to give you something beautiful, too," I say, holding the necklace out to her.

"A goodbye gift," I add as Emma traces her fingers on the delicate chain.

"It is... it is so lovely. Thank you," she whispers.

"May I? I ask her.

"Yes," Emma replies, nodding, as I place the chain around her neck, and a rush of emotions floods my body. She looks down at the necklace, admiring its intricate design and how it catches the light.

"It looks beautiful on you," I say, stepping back, fixing my eyes on the necklace and how it shimmers against Emma's skin.

Emma touches the necklace, feeling its weight against her chest.

"Thank you," she says softly as her eyes meet mine.

"I just wanted to give you something special," I say, my voice filled with tenderness.

"You always know how to make me feel special," she replies.

We sit by the fountain, running water soothing our worries.

"Emma, I need to tell you something," I say softly.

"What is it?" Emma asks me, turning towards me with a hint of concern.

"I... I think I'm falling for you," I say hesitantly after deep breathing.

"Really, Max?" Emma asks me as my heart skips a beat. The intensity of her gaze is just too much to bear.

"Yeah... I mean, I am starting to feel things for you that I do not feel with anyone else," I say. "And it scares me," I add.

"Why does it scare you?" Emma asks me with a gentle voice.

I look down at our intertwined hands, my fingers tracing circles on hers.

"Because I've been hurt before," I say with my voice barely above a whisper. "And I do not want to go through that again."

"It is ok, Max. Everyone goes through it. It is not only you who had a bitter past. Everyone has it, but giving up on love is not the solution," she says, trying to console me.

"I understand, Max, that it might not be easy for you. But you do not have to be afraid of me," she says.

"What do you mean?" I ask, my voice full of uncertainty.

"I mean that... I feel the same way. I'm falling for you, too, Max," she says, confessing her love and sending joy through my whole body.

"You are?" I ask, my voice filled with wonder.

"Yes, I am. And I know that it is scary, but I also know that it is worth it. Because being with you makes me happier than anything else," she says, and a sense of relief washes over me as I look at her, my heart full of love.

"Thank you... Thank you for being here with me, for understanding me," I say, feeling grateful for the maturity that Emma showed. I lean over, kissing her passionately as she eagerly replies by swirling her tongue inside my mouth. This kiss is an indication of our newfound love. Her soft and tender lips against my skin, as our bodies radiate heat, intensifying the moment's passion. The fountain is a marvel. The sound of falling water drowning out all other sounds, as if the water seems to glow with a life of its own. The moonlight bounces off its surface in a kaleidoscope of colors as we take in the captivating beauty of the surroundings.

"Let's take a picture to mark the happiness of our love," Emma says as we capture the moment's beauty in the camera lens, heading out to the hotel.

"Max, we're having an amazing time here, but what happens when we return home? It is our last night here," Emma asks.

"I know it won't be easy. But I also know that I do not want to let you go. Not now, not ever," I reply.

"I feel the same way, Max. I do not want this to end," she replies with sincerity in her voice.

"Then let's make a promise to each other," I say, taking her hand, my voice full of determination.

"What?" she asks.

"Let's promise that we'll give this a chance. Even when we're apart, even when it gets hard. Let's promise to fight for each other," I say.

"I promise. I promise to fight for us, to give this a chance. Even when it is hard, even when it hurts." Emma repeats back my words. I can feel the depth of our love in her voice.

I pull her into my arms, holding her tight against my chest.

"Thank you for being here with me, for giving me a chance," I say as we continue walking, discussing the challenges ahead and the difficulties of maintaining a relationship long distance. But through it all, we remain committed to each other, determined to make it work.

"I know it won't be easy. But I also know that it will be worth it. Because you're worth it,

Emma," I say as we approach our hotel, feeling sadness settling over me. Our time in Denver is ending, and we will soon say goodbye. But I also know that this was just the beginning, that our relationship is only just starting to blossom.

"Max, I do not want this to end," she says.

"It doesn't have to end. We can make this work, Emma. I know we can." I say with my voice full of hope.

As we part, I feel a sense of hope and joy washing over me. I know this relationship will be challenging, and there will be bumps ahead. But I also know that anything is possible with Emma by my side. And as we say our goodbyes, I realize this is only the beginning of my and Emma's beautiful love story.

CHAPTER 10

Going home

EMMA

"Finally, the competition is over," I say to Max as we both head out of the building. As finalists, we had to give interviews to the press and make promotional videos to be used in the next year's competition. Since I was the winner, my interviews had been much longer than Max's. I didn't mind, though.

"Yeah, it was enjoyable, though. I am going to miss it," Max says to me.

"Oh yeah? What was your favorite part?" I ask him.

"Meeting you," he says to me. Gosh, he is just so smooth at times. I can't handle it.

I start blushing and look at Max. He is looking at me with a warm smile.

"I am happy, too, you know, that I met you and we got to be with each other," I tell him. He kisses my head.

"I am going to miss this," he says.

"Yeah, me too," I tell him.

"You know what I was thinking?" Max stops and looks at me.

"What?" I ask him.

"How about we have a date together before we go our separate ways this evening?" he asks me. We both have evening flights home.

"That is a lovely idea, Max," I tell him.

"Alright then, we are going for an early dinner tonight. I will pick you up at four p.m."

"I can't wait for it," I tell him.

"Me too. Now give me your number," he says as he slides me his phone.

"Here." I put my number in his phone. "Call me," I say as I wink at him.

"Gladly," he says as he smirks and pulls me in for a deep kiss.

I head back to my hotel room, grateful for my extremely late check-out, and decide to wear my favorite outfit. My royal blue dress that is somewhere between a day dress and an evening look. Then, I catch up all my friends and family on my experiences that past week.

Time isn't passing by quickly, and I do not know why. I just can't wait for it to be four p.m. so I can see Max. I miss him. As I am thinking about him, I get a call from him.

"Missing me already, I see," I answer the call and tease him.

"Yeah, I think it is really unfair that I have to see you at four p.m. and then say goodbye to you at nine, and then god knows when I will see you again," Max says in that tone he has.

"Yeah, I was thinking about the same thing," I tell him.

"Oh yeah? Then come on outside. I am waiting for you. Wear comfortable shoes. It's gorgeous out and I want to walk a little bit," he says to me.

"I'll be right out," I tell him.

I go out and run over to Max as he hugs me.

"Where are we going?" I ask him.

"To get an Americano," he says, and we both laugh. That was the day when we both fell for each other but didn't really know about each other's feelings, so we kept it to ourselves. Max told me later how he was going to confess his attraction to me, but I left, and I have regretted it ever since. If I had stayed, maybe we would have had more time together.

Max and I head to the coffee shop together, then he takes me to the lakeside, and we feed the ducks. We later head to a bench to watch the ducks swim.

"Oh, it is so beautiful," I say as I look at the late afternoon orange sunlight melting in the clouds and giving it an ethereal look.

"I know, and I love that I am watching this with you," he says to me.

"Me too," I say as I look over to him and kiss his cheek.

I grab my phone from my pocket and turn the camera on.

"You took so many pictures today. What are you doing now?" Max asks me.

"Making memories," I say to him as I kiss him, and he smiles.

"We are going to be in a long-distance relationship starting tomorrow, Max. I want to make as many memories as I can," I tell him.

"I do not even want to think about tomorrow right now. I just want to enjoy this moment here with you right now," he says to me.

I put my head on his shoulder and grab his hand.

Max and I sit in silence for a while, looking at the sunset. It makes me sad not knowing when we will sit like this again and watch the sunset together. I hate the idea of not seeing him every day.

It is almost time for our dinner reservations.

"Come on, or we are going to be late for dinner," Max says as he gets up and gives me his hand.

"Do we have to go? I mean, we can just have a lovely time by ourselves," I ask him.

"You are going to love this place," he says to me, and I get up and hold his hand as we walk together.

Max takes me to a building where our competition was held.

"I do not remember a restaurant here. Why are we here?" I ask him out of confusion.

"Just wait and follow my lead," Max says as he grabs my hand and takes me to the building's rooftop.

We get to the rooftop, and Max puts his arms around my eyes so I can't see anything.

"Uh, what are you doing, Max?" I laugh.

"Just wait," he says softly in my ear.

We walk a few steps further, and then he removes his hands from my eyes. "Surprise," he says as he points to a small table with two chairs next to a barbecue grill. The whole rooftop is decorated with flowers and fairy lights.

I gasp. "When did you do all this?" I ask him.

"Today, it didn't take me that long. I just wanted to make our last moments here memorable for us," he says to me as I walk over to him.

"I love it," I say softly as I kiss him. "Thank you for this," I tell him.

"Come on, time to cook," he says as he grabs an apron and gives me a chef's hat.

We both laugh and have fun together as we cook and play around. Cooking is how we met, and I like the idea of spending our last night together doing what we love.

Max and I have a wonderful time cooking dinner and then eating it together on the beautiful rooftop that he has decorated for me.

I pour wine into my glass and walk around the rooftop, looking around and admiring the effort that he put into this.

Max walks over to me and grabs my hand.

"I do not want this night to be over," he says to me.

"Me either. I do not want to leave," I tell him.

"Should we go in my room and have one last moment together?" he asks.

"Let's go," I smile.

As we enter his room, I look into his eyes, and I notice his eyes locked on my lips.

"What are you looking at?" I ask, breaking the silence.

"Your beautiful lips," he replies seductively, coming so close to me that I can feel his warm breath on my face.

"They will be even more beautiful if..." I start saying when he crushes his lips on my lips doing exactly what I want to say. It seems like we can read each other's minds. I was craving his body and seeing him standing only in his boxers is turning me on. We break the kiss, trying to catch our breaths.

"You look hot," I say with my breathless voice.

"You too," he replies with a smile after undressing me completely and coming over to me placing his erected cock against my wet center.

"Just get in me, Max," I say, my sassy side coming out.

"Wait a little, baby girl," he says as he starts kissing me on my neck, tilting my neck up seductively. He grabs my waist, entering into my pussy, giving gentle and light strokes. A soft moan leaves my mouth as he immediately places his lips onto mine, shutting me down.

His sexy body, his moves, his touch. I think to myself when he thrusts it again, taking me out of my fantasies. Our bodies slap together as we come out of our ecstatic world the moment our cum leaves our body.

"Emma. You mean so much to me," Max says, making me realize how lucky I am to have him in my life.

I have time to lay with him before we catch our separate flights back home. I smile contently, seeing Max's peaceful expression as he sleeps with his chin on my shoulder, his arms engulfing me. I can feel his leg intertwined with mine as if he was scared that I might run away if he didn't wrap me around himself completely. He is holding me so tightly, even in his sleep, that I can't move, so I decided to stay there and make the most of the time I have left with him.

"You could take a picture, so you stare at me as much as you want, whenever you want," he says suddenly, without opening his eyes.

I shove him a little as I realize he has been up all this time and has been pretending to be asleep.

"Why should I take a picture when I can look at the real thing. Plus, can I do this with a picture?" I say softly before peppering his face with kisses affectionately. His laugh as I pepper kisses on his cheeks and nose warms my heart, and I want this moment to pause, for it to never pass. I wish I could just stay here, at this moment, in his arms, where we are both happy.

When I finally pull back, we both stare into each other's eyes, communicating with them how hard saying goodbye is. His eyes soften as he sees tears well up in my eyes and pulls me close to him until my head is on his chest and I am hugging him.

"We should get up. We both have flights to catch," I whisper into his chest.

"Just five more minutes," he says.

We stay like that for a few minutes, wrapped up in each other's arms, before we finally break apart and start collecting our things.

Before we know it, we are standing at the airport holding hands. His flight is supposed to take off fifteen minutes before mine.

"Flight 2718, Denver to New York. Please proceed towards the boarding area." We hear the announcement.

My eyes instantly well up with tears. This is it. This is the moment I have been dreading. Saying goodbye to Max is the hardest thing ever, and I am not ready for it.

"Emma, it is okay. We will stay in touch. Please do not cry. I can't bear the sight of your tears," he says as he wipes away my tears before leaning down to press a soft kiss to my lips.

I stand up on my toes and deepen the kiss, wrapping my arms around his neck, and I express with my kiss what I can't with my words.

Five minutes later, I finally calm down a little and wave at Max as he leaves for his flight. As soon as he disappears, the announcement for my boarding is also made, and within the next few minutes, I am sitting on the plane, too, waiting for takeoff.

I can't help but miss Max already. The past few days I have become so accustomed to his presence that I feel like something is missing from my life now that he isn't here. But I try to put these sad thoughts aside and think about my mom. I can't wait to get back and tell her everything.

After my dad left us for the sake of his popularity and career, it has just been my mom and me. My mom is my biggest supporter. She is the one who has been there for me every second of my life. No matter what I needed, she always provided me with it. And I want nothing more than to make her proud. And I could not wait to see her again.

I spend the rest of the flight sleeping and only wake up when the plane is about to land. The moment I step out of the airport, I scan the sea of faces for the familiar heart-shaped face of my mom. My eyes instantly catch her brown hair that cascades down her back as she squeals in excitement when she sees me. I run towards her and instantly engulf her in a hug.

"Oh, baby, I missed you so much!" she says as she hugs me tight.

"I missed you too, Mom," I say as we pull back.

I take out my medal for winning the competition and show it to her, and she smiles as her eyes gloss over with tears.

"Have I ever told you how proud I am of you?" she says as she looks at my medal.

"Yes, you have. Everyday," I say with a fond smile.

We make small talk as she asks me a million questions about my stay in Denver, and I entertain her with all the details. When we are both seated in the car, she asks me, "So, what's the plan now?"

"I am going to use this money that I won to open my own cupcake bakery. I need your help," I tell her confidently.

This is my dream, and winning this competition is just the first step. I will prove to my father that I am more capable than he ever imagined.

CHAPTER 11

Back to Reality

MAX

As I walk away from Emma, I feel a sense of hollowness settle over me. I want nothing more than to just turn around and walk back towards her, wrap her in my arms, and never let her go again. But I know that is not an option. We have to go our separate ways. That has always been the plan. *Then why does it feel like I am ripping out my own heart with my bare hands as I walk away from her?*

I board the plane, my thoughts still consumed by Emma's tear-filled eyes as we said our goodbyes. I still can't get over the fact that I woke up so many times the past week with Emma peacefully sleeping in my arms. At that moment, everything was perfect. I was happy, and my life was perfect. And now I am walking away from all of that. Just like that.

Leaving Emma feels like I am leaving a piece of my heart behind because the truth is that I will never be the same after this trip to Denver. It has changed me, and I never want to go back to the work-obsessed person I was before I met Emma. It doesn't matter that we barely spent a week with each other there, nor does it matter that we were always aware of how temporary this thing between us would be. To be entirely honest, when Emma and I met and were together, every obstacle and complication that existed seemed to fade away, as if it didn't even matter. As long as we were together, we could ignore the bitter truth. But now, as I sit in my seat on the plane, waiting for it to take off and take me back to New York City, thousands of miles away from Emma, the full force of loneliness crashes into me.

In the past few days, I have grown so used to the company Emma provides me with, filling the silence with her bright and cheery chatter. And now that I no longer have her sweet and soft voice filling the silence or in my head, I feel more alone than I have in ages. Ever since my mom passed away, I mostly kept to myself. I learned to fake it with people in order to be popular. I grew so accustomed to putting on a mask and acting like someone I am not. I lived a calm and peaceful life, only letting in my one close friend, Sebastian. Now that Emma is no longer by my side, I feel a sense of loneliness settle over me, making my heart constrict.

To get my attention away from the depressing thoughts running through my head, I decide to put my headphones on and listen to some songs. As soon as I put it on, the first song that plays is 'Call it what you want' by Taylor Swift, and I am instantly struck with a strong wave of nostalgia. My thoughts are transported back to the time when Emma and I spent time together, listening to our favorite songs. I remember how lively and enthusiastic she was about the whole ordeal.

~~~

FLASHBACK

"Come on, you have to have a favorite song. There must be some song you like!" she said, trying to convince me to tell her my favorite song.

"I told you. I don't have time to pay much attention to music. Work keeps me busy," I tell her with a shrug.

I watch as her lips pull into a slight pout, making my heart melt, so I lean in and kiss her pout. Before I know it, the kiss deepens, and she is in my lap as we make out, and my hands roam around her body, cherishing every part of her. Kissing her has slowly become my favorite thing to do.

Before we can take things further, Emma pulls away from me and playfully glares at me, which makes me smile. Why is she so adorable?

"You can't just distract me with a kiss, mister. You have to tell me your favorite song! I won't leave you alone until you do," she huffs, folding her arms stubbornly.

I lean back on the couch, pulling her down with me until we are both sprawled on the couch with my arms wrapped around her.

I sigh and finally answer her pestering question: "When I was young, I used to love listening to Taylor Swift," I mumble, not liking the fact that I had to share this part of my childhood with her.
~~~

She turns to look at me, her eyes widening at my answer before she breaks out, laughing her ass off. "You liked Taylor Swift?" she blurts out in between her uncontrollable laughing, making me roll my eyes, pretending to be annoyed.

"See! This is why I didn't want to tell you. I knew you would make fun of me. Plus, what's wrong with a guy liking Taylor Swift? You are such a sexist," I say defensively, huffing, even though seeing her laugh only made me happy.

"No, no, I am not making fun of you, I swear," she says, still unable to control her laughter.

I raise my eyebrows at her, and she quickly sobers up with a little bit of effort.

"It's just that I could not imagine you as someone who liked Taylor Swift, and no, I am not being sexist. It's just that she isn't your vibe," she finishes even though her statement sounds more like a question, making me chuckle.

But I do understand what she means, so I nod understandingly. She isn't wrong. I definitely do not look like someone who would listen to sappy romantic songs written by Taylor Swift, but I had my reasons. "Yeah, well. My mom used to love Taylor Swift. She used to be so excited every time she released a new album and anything that my mom loved, I loved. When I used to spend time with her, and we were in the kitchen, and she was teaching me to cook and bake, she used to play her songs and make us both dance and sing along to them, and eventually, with time, she grew on me. Every time I hear her songs now, I am reminded of my mom," I explain, my voice softening at the memories of my mom and the time we spent together.

Emma's eyes soften at the mention of my mother. She says, "She sounds like a wonderful and smart woman and an even more amazing mother."

"She really was, you know? She was the best mother I have ever seen any kid have. She loved me so much. Even on her deathbed, I was the only person she thought of, not herself, me." I tell her, my voice full of emotions.

~~~

I am pulled out of my thoughts when I notice the stewardess trying to get my attention.

"Sir, would you like something to drink?" she asks me as I try to pull my disoriented self back together.

I shake my head at her, dismissing her, and then lean my head back, resting it on the comfortable seat behind me. I close my eyes to fall asleep, hoping to see Emma in my dreams.

<div align="center">***</div>

It has been two weeks since I returned from Denver, and the busy life I lead in New York sucks me in right away. The day I landed, the first place I went was my restaurant, and instantly got back to work. It wasn't that I missed work or anything. It is just that if I hadn't occupied myself, I would have spent every second of my time thinking about Emma and dwelling on the what ifs of our circumstances, and I had no intentions of driving myself crazy with those thoughts, knowing that nothing good would come out of it. The bitter truth is that we are miles away,
~~~

and nothing will change this reality. It is best I do not overthink it.

I am the head chef in my restaurant and went right back into my old life before the competition, where I didn't even get enough time to use my phone or reply to texts. But somehow, thoughts of Emma still find their way into my head, reminding me of her laugh and her sweet voice. No matter how long it has been or how busy I get throughout the day, I still can't keep her out of my head. I miss her so much that sometimes it hurts me to even think of her. I miss the way her eyes light up when she saw something new, something that intrigued her. It could be something as magnificent as a glass tower or something as mundane as a kitten, but her reaction will always be the same gasp of awe. I missed how every time she laughed, my heart warmed, and it made me feel like everything was alright. She is a magnet for me, and everything else fades away when she is around. Even when she is not here, she is in my thoughts, never leaving me alone.

Days pass by, and the thought of her never leaves my mind. Everything around me reminds me of her.

The other day I was walking past a small coffee shop and saw a little girl looking at a stand of cotton candy with so much longing that I could not help but laugh. It seemed if she didn't get that cotton candy, everything would be ruined, and she would never be happy again. Seeing that little girl reminded me of the time when Emma and I were taking a stroll and came across a cotton candy stand. The way Emma's eyes lit up was so amusing. She was like a kid on Christmas Eve. She had dragged me to that food stand despite my complaints and arguments, trying to tell her how unhealthy it was. But nothing could deter her. When Emma made up her mind, she was a force to be reckoned with. She proved that to me the day she won the competition, and it is one of the things I like the most about her.

When she had taken her cotton candy, she ate it up so quickly and enthusiastically as if it were the most delicious thing in the world. I shook my head at her childish behavior but didn't say anything.

Looking at this little girl reminded me of Emma.

I walk towards the cotton candy stall and buy the biggest and pinkest cotton candy available there, the same one the little girl was eyeing. I pay the guy and walk towards the little girl, realizing that now it is me who she is eying enviously. A small laugh escapes me at that; her eyes widen comically as she realizes that I am walking straight toward her, and she quickly turns to her mom, trying to appear innocent.

I walk towards them and tap her mom on the shoulder with a soft smile on my face.

"Hey, do you mind if I talk to your daughter for a second?" I asked her politely. She looks at me suspiciously for a second but sees something that reassures her, and she nods.

I bend down until I am at the same level as the little girl, who is looking up at me with wide eyes.

"Hi, what is your name?" I ask her

"Anna, but I swear I wasn't staring at you! I promise I was just looking at the cotton candy." She blurts it out instantly, making her mother laugh.

"I know that. You really like cotton candy that much?" I ask her

"Yes! It's the best sweet ever." She says it enthusiastically, once again reminding me of Emma.

I hand her the cotton candy, but she hesitates to take it, looking up at her mom for approval. When she nods, she takes it from me tentatively and asks me.

"For me?"

I nod at her and reply, "For you."

She jumps in excitement and hugs my leg before all her attention is diverted to ravishing the candy. I am about to turn when her mother stops me.

"That was a very nice thing you did. But can I ask you why?" she asks

I turn around and, with a soft smile on my face, say, "She reminded me of someone very special to me." I say this and turn to leave.

Somehow, no matter where I am, I find myself linking everything to her.

As I walk around the city, I take in the chattering crowds on the streets of New York City. The aroma of melted cheese and grilled burgers infiltrates my nostrils. I am in the middle of a hundred people, and yet I feel alone. The only time I didn't feel alone was when Emma was by my side.

As I walk past people, I come to a stop when I see a small cupcake shop. Seeing the red velvet cupcakes on display transports me back to the time in Denver when Emma baked them as one of her practice bakes. But we never got the chance to eat them because, before we knew it, her lips were pressed against mine, and we were headed toward our bedroom.

Seeing this feels like the final straw, and I finally snap. I am unable to deal with the hollowness I feel inside me due to her absence. I pulled out my phone.

I book the first flight I find to her hometown, Sutton.

Was this an impulsive decision? Yes.

Did I regret it? Not at all.

Emma has a big surprise coming her way. Let's hope she is ready to handle it. I give myself a small smile.

CHAPTER 12

Reunion

EMMA

I enter the small shop, taking another lap around its interior, trying to visualize how I would make the barren space into a bakery. The place was small but not narrow. It was actually the perfect size for the kind of shop I had in mind for the small, cozy bakery I had always dreamed of opening. I would have to paint this place in soft, neutral colors to create a calm and serene environment for my customers and make sure that they felt at ease when they were here. When I was a kid, I searched this entire town for a place to relax and let go, somewhere I could just exist and not have to deal with any problems.

But the only place here that provided us with even a semblance of peace was our local library, which was a small building brimming with books you would lose yourself in. I hid out there most days when I wanted to escape the brutal remarks my father had dished out to me. It was then that I decided that I would be the one to open up a shop where people could just relax for a moment, where they could let go of their worries and troubles and just be themselves.

I am busy trying to put my thoughts in order and trying to think of ways to design this new shop I bought, and a million ideas run through my head. There is a lot to do right now. I am well aware of that, but I am just not sure where to start. The money I won from winning the Fire and Flame competition is safely stashed away, along with my other savings. Opening this bakery has always been a dream, and I have been saving up for it since I was sixteen. Now, at this point, I have enough savings to open my bakery without having to worry about my finances, which I am grateful for. I am busy trying to measure the walls of the small shop for the size of the counter that I have to order when my phone rings. Without looking at the contact, I answer the call, unaware of who's on the other end.

"Hello?" I answer, still lost in my thoughts.

"How far are you from the airport?" I hear a deep, familiar voice drawl from the other side, making my heart suddenly beat too fast.

"Max!?" I exclaim, unable to process whatever is going on.

"Emma," he replies, and I can hear the smile in his voice. "All I want to know is if you can pick me up from the airport or should I call a car?" He says it conversationally as if this were just another normal conversation we have every day, not as if this is the first time we are talking since we said goodbye in Denver.

"Are you saying what I think you are saying?" I ask him, trying my best to contain the excitement in my voice just in case this is a cruel joke he is playing on me. If that is the case, I would personally kill him and bury him.

"That depends. Do you think I'm standing at the airport in Sutton, talking to you, and waiting for your answer? Then yes, I'm saying what you think I'm saying," he says sarcastically, and a huge grin appears on my face.

"You sly little...! Don't you dare move from there. I'm coming to get you in five minutes!" I shouted excitedly as I rushed towards my car, unable to control my enthusiasm any longer.

We disconnect the call, and I rush towards the airport, forcing myself not to break the speed limit.

I can't believe it. I want to pinch myself to make sure this isn't a dream. And yes, it is embarrassing to even recount the number of times I have dreamed about this, but that's not important. What is important is that Max is really here for me. God, this has to be a dream.

The past two weeks have not been easy for me. I miss Max so much that on most nights, I cry myself to sleep just because I have gotten used to the feeling of sleeping in his arms, and suddenly sleeping in an empty bed seems like a punishment for a crime I didn't even commit. No matter where I went, I was haunted by the memory of our times together. I couldn't let them go, nor could I keep them and torture myself.

Every time I saw a couple together, going on cute dates and kissing on the sidewalk, strolling around holding hands, I wanted to cry because I used to have that with Max when we were in Denver, and now I had nothing but the memories of our good times together.

It doesn't matter how temporary all of that was. All that matters is that it was the most memorable thing I have ever experienced. The moments I have spent with Max have truly felt like a dream come true, like a fairytale. Everything was just so perfect.

But like every dream, this one also had to come to an end when we went our separate ways after the competition. Leaving Max was like breaking my own heart. I do not even remember if I was this upset when my father left. Maybe that is because I had lost respect for my father. By the time he finally left us, I was mature enough to know that it was a good thing rather than a bad thing. We were finally getting rid of a toxic person who only considered himself in his decisions. But with Max, it is different. He is simply one of the best people I have ever met.

But now Max is here, and I could not wait to see him.

The minute I reach the airport, I park my car and jump out of it, rushing to the waiting area of the airport and bumping into several people. I do not stop to apologize today. I'm making a mental note to be nice to people for a week to make up for being a nuisance to them right now.

I rush inside and search for Max's familiar face in the sea of faces until my eyes connect with his, and everything else fades away.

No longer able to control my emotions now that he is in front of me, I break out into a run, wanting nothing more than to be in his arms right now. We both run towards each other until we are only inches apart, and I jump into his arms, and he catches me with a muffled "oomph," wrapping his arms around my waist tightly as I wrap my legs around him, hugging him like a koala. I do not care who is watching or where we are right now. I hold him tight, hiding my face in the crook of his neck, and inhale his familiar musky scent.

I feel his arms tighten around me as he buries his face in my hair as we both embrace each other right in the middle of the airport, uncaring of the judgmental looks the people surrounding us were throwing our way.

All I cared about was that he was here and that he was real. Being in his arms here and now made everything else feel insignificant.

As we finally pull apart, I take in his familiar features, and I feel my heart beat so hard. It feels as if this is the first time I feel alive since I left Denver.

"Hi," I whisper, finally pulling myself together.

"Hi," he says back in a soft voice.

I try to look away from his beautiful eyes, but I find myself leaning in instead, the desire visible in his eyes until our lips finally meet and the sparks fly. His arms wrapped around me, pulling me closer to him as I wrap my arms around his neck. When we finally break apart, we're both breathing heavily, our lips slightly swollen due to the intensity of our kiss, and I blush when I realize that my lipstick transferred onto his lips, so I reach out and wipe it away to the best of my ability, and we both end up laughing at the red lipstick stains he has on his mouth now.

"I missed you so much," he says as he slips his arm around my waist and starts walking us out of the airport and towards the parking lot. That is when I realize all the eyes around us were on us and our very public display of affection. I immediately flush red in embarrassment and walk out of the airport faster, making Max chuckle and try to pull me back, but I wave his arms away with an annoyed huff.

I lead him to my car, and he puts his suitcase in before settling in.

"So, can you tell me what you're doing here?" I ask him.

"If you want, I can go back," he says teasingly, making me roll my eyes.

"I missed you, and I decided to visit you," he says casually.

"Just like that?" I ask him, looking at him.

"Just like that," he says, placing a hand on top of mine and making my heart melt at his sweet words. Who would believe that this is the same asshole who bumped into me the first time we met and proceeded to accuse me of his mistake?

"So, do you want to go home, or should I take you out for a tour of my town?" I ask him.

"I'm not really tired, plus I'm famished, so let's go for lunch," he suggests.

"Sure, what do you feel like eating?" I smile.

"Something unhealthy. It has been a while since I had unhealthy food," he says after thinking for a moment.

"We have the most delicious tacos here. Wanna try them?" I offer.

"Tacos it is," he says with a smile.

As we make our way to the place that makes tacos, we share everything that has happened to us in the past two weeks. He tells me about his busy work schedule, and I tell him about the shop I bought for my bakery.

We finally reached a small taco place that is quite famous in Sutton.

"The tacos here are to die for," I say as my mouth waters at the smell of freshly cooked tacos.

We catch up for a while, eating tacos, both of us unable to control our moans at how good they taste, and then I decide to take him on a tour of my town. I take him to the local museums, along with the few parks. He even convinces me to take him to the local zoo, too. And even though I try to argue, he convinces me, and I give in. I would be lying if I said that I didn't have fun because I did. We both took turns feeding the animals, and watching Max run away from the small ducks following him was hilarious.

We took several pictures as we visited different places. My favorite picture is the one in which Max is looking down at me with an adoring smile that lit up his entire face while I have a grin on my face, and true happiness radiates from me. We hold hands and share a few sweet kisses as we tour the town and capture as many moments as we can.

When I returned from Denver, one of my biggest regrets was not taking enough pictures, and there is no way I am making the same mistake again.

It is now time for dinner, and I am taking Max back home, where my mom is waiting for us. I feel a little nervous introducing my mom to him, but I have talked about Max so much to my mom that she's as excited as I was to see him. I walk into the house, take Max's coat and my own coat, and hang them up as I announce our arrival.

"Mom, we are home!" I call out. I watch as my mom rushes out of the kitchen, still wearing an apron, completely ignores me and pulls Max into a hug. I stare at her dumbfounded for a minute, but a laugh escapes me when I see Max's awkward expression.

"Oh, I can't tell you how much I have wanted to meet you ever since Emma came back from Denver," she tells him, finally pulling back from the hug.

"I... uh." Max scratches his neck nervously, which makes me laugh louder. He turns to look at me and playfully glares at me, but I just wink at him.

"Mom, let the poor guy breathe. Come, let's sit down," I say, leading them to the dining area.

We all settle down, and my mom starts serving her homemade lasagna, and soon we are all comfortably chatting with each other.

"If you do not mind me asking, where is your dad, Emma?" Max asked hesitantly, making me halt my fork midway to my mouth.

The room falls into heavy silence as I try to find words to explain my complicated relationship with my father.

But before I can say anything, my mom answers him. "Her dad left us when Emma was just eighteen and never looked back. Apparently, fame is more important than his own kin," she says as if it doesn't bother her, but I know better.

"I'm sorry. I shouldn't have mentioned it," Max says apologetically, but my mom brushes it off.

"It is an old topic, now. I tell Emma to move on, too. Did you know she went to win Fire and Flame because her dad has never been able to win, and she wanted to prove to him that she was better than him? But none of that matters. He didn't even blink an eye when she won," my mom says bitterly.

"Mom, leave it. It doesn't matter," I say and change the topic, and soon the atmosphere is back to normal.

Seeing my mom and Max chat away makes my heart melt. I just hope this lasts.

CHAPTER 13

Obstacles

MAX

I wake up, and the first thing that registers to me is that I am not in my room. I jolt up at the realization, but I do not make it far. I look down at the arms and legs wrapped around me like a literal koala, and a smile makes its way to my face as the realization of where I am comes back to me. Last night at dinner, I made the mistake of mentioning her father, something I shouldn't have done, but I let my curiosity win. I have noticed that every time Emma mentioned her family, the mention of her father was missing.

At the thought of her father, my jaw clenched instantly. How could someone do this to a kid? How could he choose his career and his fame over his own family? Knowing that her father had abandoned her at the age of eighteen made me angrier than ever. But her mother was right. It wasn't worth it to dwell on these matters anymore. He wasn't worth it.

I am pulled out of my thoughts when I feel Emma moving in my arms, and instinctively my arms tighten around her, holding her to me as if I am scared, even in my subconscious, that she will disappear if I do not hold on tight.

"Uh, have you decided to be my jailor?" I hear a muffled noise come from where Emma is wrapped up in my arms, and a surprised chuckle escapes me at her words.

"Depends," I say.

"On what?" she asks, resting her chin on my chest and looking up at me with those beautiful eyes of hers.

"On whether you plan on escaping or not," I tell her, and it is now her turn to laugh.

She leans up and drops a sweet kiss on my lips in response.

She tries to pull away after a few seconds, but I do not let her. I deepen the kiss, my tongue demanding entrance. The moment my tongue enters her mouth, she moans into the kiss, even as I ravage her mouth.

Somewhere in our making out, Emma ends up straddling me, her hips rocking onto mine as she starts grinding on me. I wrench my lips from hers and start trailing kisses down her neck. My desire for her is evident by the bulge in my boxers.

I slide her panties down, leaning over her and crushing my lips onto hers, as we savor the taste of each other.

"Emma, you really turn me on," I say, and I smile slightly, slipping my boxers down as my cock springs free.

"Are you ready?" I ask her with a half-smirk on my face, as she buries her face in my chest. I can feel her face getting flushed as I tickle her clitoris with my dick.

"Yeah!" she says nodding, as I thrust it with full force inside her pussy.

"Give a little warning at least!" she says, and I smile widely, thrusting my cock in and out of her pussy. I grab her hips, rocking them back and forth as I move my lips inside her mouth with the movement of my cock. We both come close to orgasm, feeling ecstatic, lost in our small world of love and passion. I pull it out, as we both start dripping. We both sit there breathless, smiling after this intense lovemaking that reminds us that we both are meant to be together.

I lie down in bed again with a content sigh.

"God, I missed this so much," I tell her as we both catch our breath.

"Really? Should I assume that this is the only reason why you miss me?" she says mockingly.

"Maybe," I reply with a smirk.

"Oh my god! Now I know why you came here unannounced! You came here for this, didn't you?" she says, narrowing her eyes at me, and I can no longer hold back my laughter as I bust out laughing, and soon she joins me, too.

I kiss her forehead gently as I get up. "I came back because you are the only one I think of enough to miss. The amazing sex is just a bonus," I throw over my shoulder as I walk over to the bathroom and clean up, and then I wet a towel and bring it out with me.

I walk over to her, and she raises her eyebrow at the towel in my hand, and I just motion for her to stay put as I clean her up.

"I am going for a shower. Do you want to join?" I ask suggestively, which earns me a pinch on my arm.

"If I step inside that shower with you, I won't come out anytime soon, so no, you go alone. And hurry up! We have a lot to do today," she says, and I give her a confused look.

"Like what?" I ask her.

"All in good time. Do not be impatient. Now, go!" she says as she is pushing me towards the door, but I sneakily wrap my arm around her waist and throw her over my shoulder, making her shriek as I walk us both into the bathroom.

And she was right—we won't make it out of there anytime soon.

***

Emma and I walk down the stairs and into the dining area of her house together and find her mom already seated there, the table full of things for breakfast.

"Good morning," Emma and I greet her in unison as we take a seat at the table and start piling up our plates with food.

"Good morning. Did you guys sleep well?" she asks us with a mischievous glint in her eyes that makes Emma flush, but I maintain my expression and just politely say yes, even though I am aware of what she is hinting at.

Emma and her mother have a unique bond that is less like a mother-daughter duo and more like best friends. They seem to understand each other well without even having to communicate and seeing them like this reminds me of my own mother.

Would it be like this with me and my mom, too, if she had been alive today? The thought comes up in my head as I witness them both happily chatting away, but not allowing myself to wallow, I brush it aside and focus on Emma.

"So, what's the plan for today?" I ask Emma once we are done having breakfast, and I watch as her eyes light up with excitement.

"We are going for a picnic!" she announces excitedly.

"A picnic?" I ask her.

"Yes! We have the most beautiful hills here, and the drive is only fifteen minutes. The sunset there is the most beautiful thing ever. And that's not even the best part. We are both going to cook our best dishes and take those along with us." She continues explaining the plan to me, and I can see how excited she is, making me smile.

"So, what do you want me to make?" I ask her.

"Hmm..." she says as she ponders over it. "Oh, I know! I have heard that your Alfredo pasta is to die for. Why not make that?" she suggests, and I nod my head, having no objections.

"And what will you be making?" I ask her.

"I am baking brownies!" she exclaims.

We spend the next few hours in the kitchen as we make our dishes, and around five in the evening, an hour or two before sunset, we set out for our picnic.

When we reach there, we set up the entire place and settle down, talking between ourselves until the sun finally starts setting, and Emma was right. It is the most beautiful sight ever. The sky is a rainbow of colors: orange, yellow, and red. We both sit there and watch as the sun sets until we finally pack up our things and leave.

***

I spent two days at Sutton with Emma, exploring the town, meeting people in her neighborhood, going on cute picnic dates, and stealing kisses whenever we could. Ever since I came back from Denver, I always felt like there was a part of me that was empty, as if I had left it back in Denver.

Being here, in Sutton with Emma makes me realize that I had left a part of me with her, and now that we are together again, everything feels perfect, surreal even.

But I can't help but realize that the kind of life Emma leads is very different from my own. She lives in a small town where everyone knows everyone else, no matter where they live.

She lives in a small house with her mom, living a minimalistic life, while I lead a luxurious life as the owner of one of the most well-known restaurants in New York with money to spare. Emma lives in a two-bedroom house. I live in a penthouse alone that is twice as big as her house. She travels on bicycles, even though she does have a car, but I am used to the comfort of SUVs and drivers.

She took over an hour to show me all her plans for opening a bakery. It reminded me of how excited I was to open my first restaurant. I felt more glad than ever that she had won the baking competition. But when I asked her about her plans to grow the bakery or open it in a larger place like New York, she didn't seem to want to do that. She was pure hearted and simple in her tastes, very unlike me.

Emma and I could not be any more different from each other even if we tried, and yet none of that matters when I am with her. She makes me feel something I have never experienced with another girl. But could it even work out between us?

These are the thoughts running through my head on my way to the airport while Emma continues to chatter animatedly, not noticing my distant expression.

When we finally reach each other, I realize that this is the second time we are saying goodbye to each other. But somehow, it is even more challenging and a million times more hurtful this time around. But I put on a brave face and kiss her goodbye.

"Do not miss me too much, okay?" I tease her, even though I am barely keeping my own emotions in check. I can see the tears shining in her eyes, and I know that I will not be able to handle her crying right now. So, I do not linger. I hug her one last time and leave without turning back even once.

When I am seated on the plane, I take a calming breath. *I will not cry.* I repeat this line in my head like a mantra until the tears in my eyes settle and the intense need to cry passes. I decided to go to sleep. Knowing that if I stay up, I won't be able to pull myself together.

***

I am woken up by the stewardess when the plane is about to land, and I take a moment to adjust to my surroundings. Everything I tried to forget by going to sleep comes back to me, and suddenly I am wide awake again.

When I walk out of the airport, my driver is waiting for me. I walk towards my car and settle in.

"Where to, sir?" he asks me, and I consider it.

I want to go home, but the thought of going back to an empty home and sleeping in an empty bed after having Emma sleep in my arms for the past two days makes my heart constrict. I could go to the restaurant, but I do not feel like working, either.

My heart is in too much of a dilemma for me to be able to focus on anything else right now.

I am so conflicted about this thing with Emma. What do I even do? I really need to talk to someone about this, but who?

That's when I remember the one person who has always had my back. I want to face palm myself for taking so long to think of him.

"Take me to Sebastian's house," I tell my driver.

Sebastian Collier is my one and only friend. He and I met in high school, and even though we never went ahead with the sappy notion of claiming to be each other's best friend, we had both stuck together over the years, having each other's back whenever we needed it. Every time one of us was in trouble, the other came to the rescue, and I knew that only he could help me right now.

Sebastian is the CEO of a large investment firm, so he is used to the same lifestyle as me, but he is one of the kindest people I have ever met. When I reach the door, I ring the bell and wait for it to open.

The door opens, and a timid-looking maid stands behind it. She instantly recognizes me and stumbles to open the door and let me in.

"Sir, Mr. Collier wasn't expecting you. Please wait in the living room. He will be down shortly," she says primly, but I cut her off.

"It's all right. Just tell him I'm waiting for him in the living room," I tell her calmly, not wanting to loiter in the entryway any longer.

She nods and rushes to inform Sebastian of my arrival. I walk into the living room and settle down, waiting for him.

Ten minutes later, Sebastian walks into the room, confusion evident on his face due to my unannounced arrival.

"Max, is everything okay?" he asks in a concerned voice.

"Yes, yes. Everything is all right." I tell him, willing him to calm down.

"What are you doing here?" he asks, taking a seat opposite me.

"I need to talk to someone," I tell him.

"Is everything okay?" he repeats.

"I'm just so conflicted, man," I groan, and I proceed to tell him everything that happened in Denver and everything about Emma.

"I don't know what to do, man. There are so many conflicts and things to work through. She lives a completely different life than me, not to mention that she is eleven years younger than me. There is so much she has yet to experience," I tell him with a sigh.

He takes a moment to consider everything before he answers.

"I understand that this is a difficult situation for you, but despite all these issues, do you still want to give this a shot?" he asks.

I pause, considering this question, but the answer is simple.

"Yes. Emma is everything. I never thought I would get it, but now that I have had her in my life, I can't let her go," I tell him sincerely.

He smiles at my answer. "There you go, then. Every relationship has complications, but it is the will to make things work that can make a new relationship successful."

"But how can we even try when she lives in a different town?" I ask him.

"I do not have an answer to that, but what I will say is that if you try hard enough, things will work out. But in the end, you have to be the one to make the decision," he says solemnly.

I nodded at his words. He's right. I am the one who has to make the decision. I just hope that I do not regret whatever I decide to do.

CHAPTER 14

Happily, Ever After

EMMA

I cannot believe that I am doing this, but I am on my way to book tickets to New York for this weekend. Max had visited me in my hometown a few days ago, and we had a magical time together. So, it is my turn, and I have planned to surprise him with my visit.

It is Wednesday today, and I have booked my flight for Friday. I hope to have dinner with Max after my surprise. I cannot contain my excitement, so I call him. He answers after a few rings.

"Hey, how is my girl?" he asks in a pleasant tone.

"I am good. How are you?" I reply.

"How did you know that I was missing you?" he says.

"That is because our hearts are connected," I chuckle, and he laughs, too.

"So, is there any reason behind this call?" he asks.

"Yes, I wanted to tell you that I have made my decision about the launch of my bakery because the place is almost furnished and decorated. So, I was thinking I will inaugurate it whenever you can come here. Make your plans accordingly," I tell him.

"Wait, wait, wait... I thought it is your turn to come to New York, not the other way round," he fakes sadness in his voice.

"Looks like someone is not excited," I smirk.

"Hey, no... you know I was kidding. I am so happy for this big achievement of yours. Please make sure you make your famous carrot cupcakes before the launch, so I can sneak in and have my guilty pleasure." We both laugh as he says this.

"Alright, now I've got to go. See you soon," I tell him.

"Goodbye," he drops the call.

I am smiling like a lunatic. I cannot wait to see his expression when he opens the door to see me standing in front of him.

******

It is Friday afternoon, and after finishing my projects for the weekend, I am on my way to the airport for my surprise. I know Max has a busy schedule today, but he will be free by five. So, I expect him to be at home when I reach NYC. I still cannot believe that I will be able to see him in a few hours. After his visit to my town ended, I missed him so dearly that everything looked incomplete without him. My days got so boring, and the time slowed down. But now that I am about to see him, I am ecstatic.

*****

I am in his driveway, and I can see the lights coming from one of the rooms of the house. I ring the bell with my heart beating really fast. I wait a little bit, but no one answers the door. *Maybe he is not at home, but I can see lights in there.* My overthinking starts. Anyways, I keep my thoughts aside, and I ring the bell again. This time, I hear the sound of steps as if someone is coming down the stairs. My heart is beating faster. In a few moments, I am about to see him.

The steps are coming closer now, and the door opens.

I turn around to see him. He gasps and stops right there. I go and hug him tight. He takes a moment to return to reality. And holds me tightly in his embrace. Finally, after longing for him, I am able to touch him.

My eyes are welling, we break apart, and he asks me,

"Emma... how is this possible ... how are you? ... when did you come?"

Instead of answering, I lock my lips to his. He responds by kissing me back. We hold each other tightly as we kiss. He pushes his tongue into my mouth, and I relish the moment.

After a few moments, we break our kiss. We both are breathless and are panting hard. That is when he hugs me tightly again.

"I cannot believe that I can feel you in front of me," he smiles at me.

"I landed in New York just an hour ago. I wanted to surprise you," I tell him.

"Emma, this is the best surprise of my whole life," he replies with teary eyes.

"So, you will keep me at the door," I tease him in my attempt to lighten the mood.

"Oh… it's just that I cannot contain my excitement anymore. Make yourself comfortable. I will get your bag." He leaves the door and gestures for me to come inside.

His house is sophisticatedly decorated in a way that defines the modern taste of the person living in it. Everything seems to be in its place.

He follows me in the living room and says, "Someone said she is expecting me to come to her place?"

"I still expect it. It is just that I was done decorating my shop, and I was missing you, so I thought of surprising you," I tell him.

"I love it, Emma." He leans in to kiss me again.

"Max, I am starving. Is there any chance you offer food to your guests?" I tease him.

"Oh, sorry, yes. I made pasta tonight. I will show you the washroom, freshen up, and I will dish out the food," he takes me to his room. "Make yourself at home," he smirks.

I shower and change my clothes, and when I return, I see a table beautifully decorated with candlelight and the dinner served already. Max is standing and smiling at me.

"I had no idea Mr. Chef is so quick," I comment.

"You do not have any idea about a lot of things, Ms. Baker."

We both laugh as we sit down at the table. The pasta is delicious and turns out to be as tasty as was expected. After we are done with the dinner, I help him do the dishes.

"Go to the room and get my dessert ready," he smirks.

"Oh, I am so sorry, we do not have cupcakes for dessert. Instead, I brought the baker herself," I say.

I enter the room and change into my black lace lingerie. As I am waiting for Max in the room, the large window grabs my attention. I start looking outside the window when Max comes into the room.

He pushes me to the wall, kissing me passionately, transferring all the love we both are feeling for each other right now.

"Emma, you really turn me on whenever I see you," Max says to me when we break apart from our kiss.

"It is the same with me, Max. I really want you inside me." I say, pleading with him to take me.

"Sure," Max replies with a half-smirk carrying me in his arms and taking me to the bed. He slips his jeans off, followed by slipping off my lingerie. Within seconds we both were looking at the bare bodies of each other.

"Anyone would die for your body, Emma." Max compliments me as he comes over me, putting his cock on my clitoris and spreading my legs apart.

"You want me to be gentle?" Max asks me.

"No!" I reply, looking at him in the eyes with passion oozing out from our bodies, radiating blazing heat. Max starts to give small kisses at my neck as he strokes his dick inside my pussy with full force. A loud moan escapes my mouth as he immediately crushes his lips onto mine, hiding my moans. He swirls his tongue inside my mouth, pushing his cock back and forth. I struggle to resist my orgasm when I notice a splash of white liquid drenching my thighs. I let go of my orgasm, letting go of the sheets, which I have been clenching the whole time.

"You feel so good," Max says as we both cuddle in each other's arms, enjoying the ecstasy of what we just experienced.

We embrace each other. Max seems to be in deep thought, so I ask him, "Where are you, Max?"

"Nowhere," he says mysteriously.

"Is there anything that is bugging you?" I ask again.

"I do not know Emma. You know I love you, and I love that you are here with me now, but I am thinking about the future of our relationship. My thoughts haunt me. Do we even have a future together?" he says.

I bask in his admission of love. I've known he loves me for some time, but hearing it feels natural, and right. "I love you, too. Honestly, I have been thinking about this, too. I am a small-town girl, and you live in such a big city. I do not know if we are meant for each other or not," I tell him my concerns.

"I am worried about us. I want to spend my life with you. You are the best thing that has ever happened to me, but I do not know if I am ready for a long-distance relationship. I know you have a well-settled life in your own town, and I am established here. You are even opening your own bakery very soon. Is there any place for me in your life?" he asks.

"I am here because of you, Max. I am not the same Emma that you met in Denver. I am changed, and it is you who has changed me. I cannot imagine my life without you," I tell him as I kiss his forehead.

"Are you ready to give our relationship a chance?" he looks at me hopefully.

"Yes darling, that is the only reason that I am here, with you. I want to give our relationship a real chance. I don't have all the answers figured out, but I want us to try."

"I love you," he says.

"I love you, too," I reply as I kiss his lips.

He kisses me back, and then he says, "Long distance relationships come with their own responsibilities, but I think let's give it a go and see where it takes us."

"Only if you promise that we will visit each other whenever it is feasible?" I smile.

"I cannot live without you even for a day," Max replies.

As we cuddle in the bed, the dark night, the moon, and the stars are all witness to the start of our relationship. It is a long-distance relationship whose future we have not thought of yet, but all we know is this moment. The moment that tells us that we are inseparable. Just now, I have realized the meaning of two bodies and one soul.

Max sleeps in my arms, and I cannot help myself but think about how life took us both to Denver for a cooking competition and how two strangers, who did not know about each other a few months ago, are now so close that they cannot imagine their lives without each other. This is what is known as fate.

I have to go back to Sutton and my life and establish a bakery, but I know that a part of me lives here in New York. For that part, I will return to New York soon because life has no meaning without Max, now. Thinking about this, sleep embraces me.

***

Two Years Later

I am in New York again, launching a new location of my bakery, Sprinkles. Around two years ago, Max and I decided to give this long-distance relationship a chance. And after these two years, all I can say is staying with Max was the best decision of my life that I ever made. Being with Max means happiness to me now.

In these two years, my business has grown exponentially, and I have established three locations of Sprinkles already. Much of it is because of Max's support and love for me. He has stood by me during all this time. Today is the opening of my fourth branch in the country and the first in New York.

As I am preparing for the launch, Max is eating a carrot cupcake, his all-time favorite. I cannot help but grin as I feel how this man, the greatest chef in the world, is so cute.

The launch goes well, and as I reach home after a tiring day, I see Max has filled the table with all my favorite foods. He is standing there, and as he sees me, he embraces me in a hug.

"Well done, Ms. Baker," he says.

"Thank you, I didn't know we have a celebration here," I grin.

"We have, but instead of champagne, we will celebrate with fresh juice because you should not be drinking it," he says as he caresses my belly.

"This is the best reason to not drink in the world," I say.

"Just four more months, baby," he kisses my belly as we both embrace each other again.

Our little Max is on his way. We have started building our family. We do not know what the future holds for us. All we know is that we will always be there for each other because love is what matters the most.

Chapter 15

The End

Did you like this book? Then you'll LOVE

Stuck with a Bad Boy Billionaire

– A Grumpy Enemies to Lovers Romance

I let my guard down and my bad boy billionaire boss
stepped right in

I chose to stay away from everyone after I couldn't let go of my past mistakes.

Then, Mia walked into my life, and we were forced together by a hurricane.

She should fear me, but she doesn't.

The sexual tension between us is fiery.

Oh, the things I want to do to her.

I want to hear her moan with excitement and pleasure her like she never has been before.

**Scan QR code or visit
https://www.amazon.com/dp/B0C9YDZD54
now to get *Stuck with a Bad Boy Billionaire
– A Grumpy Enemies to Lovers Romance***

Acknowledgements

To all those that have helped with my book.

Sheena
Your developmental editing perfection has been unsurpassed.

Deanna
A special thank you for all the laughs at your store –
Your friendship means the world to me.

Nadine
Thank you for the last minute help, it means everything to me.

www.ingramcontent.com/pod-product-compliance
Lightning Source LLC
Chambersburg PA
CBHW031416150726
47989CB00002B/685